TEN ACCEPTABLE ACTS OF ARSON

T0308945

TEN ACCEPTABLE ACTS OF ARSON

and other very short stories

Jack Remiel Cottrell

CANTERBURY UNIVERSITY PRESS

UNIVERSITY OF
CANTERBURY
Te Whare Wānanga o Waitaha
CHRISTCHURCH NEW ZEALAND

First published in 2021 by

CANTERBURY UNIVERSITY PRESS
University of Canterbury
Private Bag 4800, Christchurch
New Zealand
www.canterbury.ac.nz/engage/cup

ISBN 978-1-98-850325-7

A catalogue record for this book is available from the
National Library of New Zealand.

Editor: Emma Neale
Book design and layout: Gemma Banks
Cover design: Gemma Banks, using Henry Turner's painting
Simcha, gouache on paper, 2019
Printed by Caxton, New Zealand

Contents

To my mother Sharon, for dragging me this far.

Monday

12 On Monday, a man broke into my car and stole a bag of coat hangers. I know it was a man because he left a business card on the back seat. Rain had leaked through the broken window and smudged the text, apart from the name *Gary*.

Stay in school. Stay indoors. Know where your emergency exits are. Shop normally. Ensure you have three litres of treated water per person per day. Check your gas heater is properly flued. Make for the nearest high ground. Wash your hands. Open doors with your elbows. Use sanitiser after every interaction. Avoid public toilets. Brush and floss twice daily. Take a multivitamin. Go organic. Go vegan. Never eat anything with ingredients you cannot pronounce. Get enough exercise. Be home by dark. Never be alone with a stranger. Don't walk through 'that' part of town. Don't give money to beggars. Wear sunscreen. Wash your face before bed. Use a condom. Don't touch your face. Don't touch handrails. Don't touch each other. Turn off all appliances at the wall. Never shake a baby. Never leave valuables unattended. Wear a helmet. Check the safety rating. Only a fool breaks the two-second rule. Wash your hands. Stay at least two metres away from other people at all times. Maintain connections with loved ones. Stretch every hour. Reduce, reuse, recycle. Don't smoke. Don't drink alcohol. Don't drink Diet Coke. Don't drink sugary drinks. Don't drink the tap water. Lock your doors. Practise mindfulness. Be grateful. Meth: not even once. Swim between the flags. If you see something, say something. Drive to survive. Never walk on the tracks. Test your smoke alarm. Test for STDs. Save for your retirement. Keep to your local area. Duck and cover. Maintain an interior fallout room. Wrap dead bodies in plastic sheeting and label with name, date of birth, and home address before placing outside. Do not leave your dwelling without your ration card. Wash your hands.

14 I'm not a terrorist. Just bored. We only did it to see if we could.

We didn't start off with hacking. The five of us were just having fun with paint, salt, radar jammers, and burner phones. Our dumb cyberpunk haircuts were more important to us than wreaking chaos.

Turning half a Starbucks into a connectivity dead zone took weeks, and I gashed my arms running away from a security guard. We hijacked hipsters' webcams to watch the frustration, but only blocked the signal for one day.

We were the ones who painted QR codes in matte varnish on the road, slowing smart cars to 30 kph when they drove over them. That got us on the news after a couple of accidents — only minor ones. Maybe that's when it started going too far. But we angled the codes so the car would only read it if the driver was speeding.

We told ourselves we were doing the world a favour.

It was supposed to replicate a biological virus, to see how fast it spread in an unvaccinated population. People are terrible at securing their tech.

The virus used near-field communication. If your NFC was on, and you came too close to a carrier, your tech got infected. Then it transmitted the virus for two hours before it blue-screened.

We hid 'Patient Zero' — an old laptop — in a train station. The one near the hospital.

I didn't know some medical equipment uses NFC. I never thought about it. And I didn't realise how many hospital staff went through that station on the way to the ICU.

We weren't trying to kill those people — it was only a prank. Stupid kids thinking they were clever.

I swear, I never meant to hurt anyone.

Maia could only make one thing out of paper: tiny origami cranes, which an older girl at Guides taught us to fold when we were ten.

Still, I loved to watch her while she tore spreadsheet printouts into squares, folded mountains and valleys with deft fingers. She eased the birds' wings apart, her pink-gloss lips pressed to the hole in the paper, murmuring as she breathed them into life.

'What are you whispering?' I asked.

'Magic,' she replied, eyes closed.

'Does it work?'

She looked over then, from her perch on the windowsill of our bedroom, with its backdrop of grey skies and drizzle, to where I lay in bed. That look was enough to make me breathe faster.

'Well, you're here.'

Maia set the newly created crane on the sill, and joined me.

In the months following the accident, I found them everywhere. Origami cranes covered with numbers that made no sense, just like it didn't make sense that there was no more Maia. They nested in the back of the pantry, or peeked out from pockets of jeans that were now too big.

I discovered a whole flock inside the glovebox when I could bring myself to buy a new car. The paper birds spilled across the passenger seat and onto the floor, an impossible swarm lying on fake leather. I stared at the delicate beaks and curving wings until my vision blurred.

When I made it home, I carried the paper birds inside and threaded them together, careful not to tear any, my hands fumbling with the knots. I hung the string of a hundred cranes across the window. They fluttered for a moment, then came to rest, framed by the drizzle falling outside.

Reasons why I called in sick rather
than go to the mihi whakatau for
new employees last Friday

1. When I did kapa haka at primary school, one of the leaders asked us who in the group was Māori. I raised my hand and a teacher told me not to be silly.

2. When I was 11 my cousin Justine, who attended kura kaupapa, laughed at my accent after I said a karakia.

3. In my first year of uni the RA asked if anyone on our floor was Māori. When I said yes, a guy yelled 'What tribe are you from, Ngāti Ginger Ninjas?'

4. The aunties at my marae have often told me I don't know anything. I'm not sure if they're right, but I believe them.

5. Two years ago, my journalism class had a lesson on te reo Māori in the news. We prepared our mihi, but when I spoke, I tried to sound more Pākehā so no one would think I was pretending to be something I'm not. Then I sat down and burned with shame.

6. Last Wednesday, I told the organiser of our mihi whakatau that I had been to pōwhiri before because I'm Māori. He laughed at me.

7. Because I didn't want another reason.

8:00 am: First dose of medications A, B, C, D, E, and F. A, B, C, and D must be taken with food. E and F cause reduced appetite. Remain upright for 30 minutes to avoid oesophageal scarring caused by medication A. Avoid exposure to sunlight due to increased photosensitivity from medications C and H (see below).

10:30 am: Second dose of B. Causes nausea.

2:30 pm: Third dose of B, second dose of D, first dose of medication G. Sip water to alleviate dry mouth from E, F, and G.

6:30 pm: Fourth dose of B, second dose of A and C. Remain upright for 30 minutes. If nausea is severe, take medication L as needed.

10:00 pm: Sole dose of medications H, I, J, and K. I, J, and K may cause excessive drowsiness; avoid driving or operating heavy machinery. If medication H produces rash, take medication M immediately.

Dx: Juvenile idiopathic arthritis, lupus, pyelonephritis, dysthymia.

Side effects may include: Tooth grinding, anxiety, weight loss, weight gain, dark coloured urine, insomnia, fatigue, peripheral neuropathy, high blood pressure, low blood pressure, stomach ulcers, constipation, dependency, nephrotic syndrome, gallstones, headache, serotonin syndrome, vivid dreams, short-term memory deficits, and retinal toxicity.

Do not stop taking this medicine without consulting your doctor.

18   Unconventional armour:
       — my nephew's grammar school hoodie
       — big headphones
       — a large book
       — the top bunk in a youth hostel dorm
       — no forwarding address.

Lavishing attention on the droids didn't bring them out of their sullen moods. So we tried to find a better term than 'robot puberty'.

Preventing the pitfalls of chrono-travel is easy. We just keep going back to stymie the inventors of time machines.

She hoped the ghosts that communicated in outlines on undeveloped Polaroids had adapted to digital cameras, but she hadn't seen any to ask.

The apprentice was told to leave room for heat expansion. But not too much, or the machinery might get ideas.

The trick isn't finding adventure,
but recognising it

Thirteen years old, you follow tracks through the bush all summer, searching for adventure.

You're at an impressionable age. Long past the *Famous Five*, you find the same themes in *Lord of the Rings* — with swordfights. You doubt you'll bump into a dragon or a wizard, but don't eliminate the possibility. You're still young enough to believe in everything.

You leave your cellphone at home. Adventures don't happen to people whose parents can call them.

You range farther every day, hunting for something close to a story in a book. You wish your sisters weren't so much older than you, that your friends wanted to spend more time outside. You wish you had more friends — enough for a gang, if not a fellowship.

The days are a search for quests, or spies, or criminals. Forget being the chosen one: you just want to be the kind of person something happens to.

Your legs are covered in scratches from hacking through brambles. Sunburn peels on your nose and neck.

When you climb trees to spy out the land, you never see anything that looks like adventure — but you do find plenty of birds, strange new mushrooms, and flowers that bloom 40 feet off the ground.

Although you feel as if your body is never the same in the morning as it was when you went to bed, you can tell you're growing stronger and faster.

If you'd been set a quest at the beginning of summer, you might have struggled. But by the time you're fit enough to swim to a cave on an island and foil smugglers, you've given up your pursuit of anything exciting.

And besides, you have to go back to school.

'What did you do in the holidays?' you ask a friend.

'Nothing. You?'

'Same.'

The most terrible assimilation is
the one we convince ourselves
is for our own good

'You don't need to do this,' said his father.

Jack reached down to release his seatbelt. He shook his head, hearing the worry in his dad's voice.

'Thanks, Dad. I'll see you at two.'

Jack didn't say that he *did* need to do this. Nor that his father should have done it for him when he was 12 years old, to make the following 12 years easier.

The clinic receptionist wore a neat uniform blouse and an equally uniform smile. She took Jack's name and date of birth, then handed him a questionnaire. Jack sat down and looked through the long list of habits that the procedure could cure.

He skipped over the 'Alcohol and Drugs' section — his flaws were more prosaic. 'Tardiness', 'Laziness', 'Untidiness', 'Procrastination' ... Check.

Behaviours like overspending, staying up all night, oversensitivity, pessimistic tendencies, lack of perseverance — he would get rid of those.

Jack also skipped over warnings about reductions in creativity, lateral thinking, and empathy. Those traits wouldn't help him get through adulthood.

The questionnaire didn't offer to fix miserliness, early-rising, perfectionism, or unwarranted optimism. No one wanted to become an idle spendthrift.

When the doctor called him, he jumped up before she even reached his second name. In 45 minutes a dozen of his worst flaws would be gone.

Jack was annoyed by ten past two, when he was still waiting for his father to pick him up. His dad was always late, and so had always excused Jack for being late.

That wasn't going to happen any more. And he wouldn't say anything this time, but when his father finally pulled in at 2:17 pm, Jack already knew he could not remain silent about these imperfections forever.

I became a geologist because I wanted to go to Mars — and stay
there. My passion for the red planet drove me through a PhD, and
the early part of my career. I'd hoped space travel would be ready
in time.

They recruited me with a cold call, a plummy voice saying there
was an opportunity for Dr Margaret Joiner. I didn't tell him that
everyone called me Maggie. I just asked what it paid.

The salary was high, but other details were scant.

'Come to a meeting,' the plummy voice urged. 'This is best
discussed in person.'

What the hell, I thought, it *was* a free trip to London.

The meeting was bigger than I'd expected — 25 people, some of
whom I knew, others whom I'd cited. Experts in biology, physics,
botany, engineering. It was impressive company.

Our potential employer was also impressive.

'This is crucial for our species,' he said. 'A bio-engineering
project none ever thought to plan for.'

'Venus?' asked one bright spark.

'No. Earth.'

A ripple passed though the room.

'I have always dreamed of space travel,' he spoke with sincerity
and a touch of sadness. 'But to see other planets, first we must save
our own.'

Bankrolled by a billionaire, with the fate of the world on the line.
I took the job.

My own dream of space has receded, now the work to terraform
Earth is under way. But I refuse to abandon it — I call it to mind in
the hours when I can't sleep.

22 Better to think of Mars than the breakthrough that eludes me. Better to stare out my window at the sky — to the stars which have never felt so distant — than risk looking back toward the clock. Toward those luminous hands, which have just ticked past midnight.

Sylvie liked data. Data, she believed, told stories in reliable ways, building   23
up over time and making plots clearer. Data had an honest narrator and
never asked for the murky interpretations that had made English classes
so unbearable.

No matter what else the company where Sylvie worked was, it was
the best. It provided services which were useful, and it provided those
services better than anyone else.

She assumed people understood that if they were getting something
for free, then they weren't the consumer, but the product.

'Our directions app consistently maps out the optimal travel route,'
Sylvie's boss told her, 'But a third of trips are abandoned or rerouted for
no obvious reason. Find out why.'

Just like that, Sylvie was a detective.

Some narratives were easy. Users terminated journeys home at nearby
stores — getting dinner. Others exited at speed, but always close to a
regular destination — the point where they no longer needed directions.

Some stories required more data, and those intrigued her. Sylvie
pulled local area information, pulled recent searches, pulled camera and
app usage.

With these she could work out what was going on in users' lives. Secret
drinkers frequented bars in neighbouring suburbs, close to home, but not
too close. Adulterers stopped in residential areas but didn't linger, and
searched for hotel rooms in the cities where they lived. Sylvie followed
people's stories through their digital breadcrumbs.

The data was anonymised — but there were ways around that. There
were ways around everything.

Sylvie sometimes imagined what she might put in a blackmail note,
if she wanted to get money fast. But as she prepared her results, she
dismissed the thought. Selling user data to advertisers paid more, and
she didn't even need an alibi.

24

1. There is a lake at the top of a mountain, where the waters are cloudy and grey. Writers catch ideas with fishing hooks — but ideas only bite if the hooks are baited with well-fed leeches.

2. The Idea Self-Recycling Programme. Originally started by Shakespeare, the programme has developed a modern format. All ideas must be rinsed and have their lids removed before recycling.

3. Theft.

4. Research, which is a more labour-intensive form of theft.

5. By sacrificing laptops or small mammals to their chosen deity under a gibbous moon.

6. Watching TV shows that are just past their prime.

7. Shamelessly repurposing events from their real lives, edited to make the writer appear more intelligent and better looking.

8. Shamelessly repurposing events from other people's real lives, yet somehow still editing them to make the writer appear more intelligent and better looking.

9. Spite.

10. Mediocre understandings of the events of history, the laws of physics, the axioms of mathematics, and the results of major sporting fixtures.

11. The tail-ends of deadlines, when the piece is two days past due.

12. Mental illness. However, most writers can't work while in the grips of mental illness, so the idea waits for therapy and/or medication.

13. Alcohol.

14. Giving up alcohol.

15. A long walk to an almost dry well. Literally. The well is 53.3 miles away from wherever the writer is. There is a bus, but it induces terrible motion sickness and the driver does not give change.

Tuesday

28   On Tuesday, I received a letter from someone claiming to be me in a
      future life. It said they had a dire warning for me, and to await further
      correspondence. The missive was written on the back of a recipe for
      French onion soup, which I do not like.

The tunnel under the train station near my house is always dark, since the fluorescent lights on the walls are enclosed in rusting steel mesh to deter vandalism. Even in the middle of the day, you have to go through night-time to reach the platforms.

There's a turf war going on down there. Faeries consider it their territory, since the strange hold of night gives the tunnel a doubly-liminal quality. Work-shy robots say they deserve exclusive use of the space, since it's a good spot to hide from drones.

Police have stopped interfering. Too many officers had their credit card details appear on the internet; or they went missing for a weekend only to turn up, alone and palely loitering, sickened by the glamour.

Jenny thought it was less dangerous for the drivers who saw the tortoise at night. The shape flashed through their headlights so fast that they didn't have time to swerve — few even jammed on their brakes. Those who did sometimes came up to the house, shaken, and asked if anyone around owned a tortoise the size of a boulder. And Jenny told them, truthfully, no.

It had been going on for years.

The drivers who saw it during the day weren't so lucky. They might brake so hard their tyres shredded, or they might swerve off the road. If they were going much over the speed limit, the driver could lose control and skid so far that their vehicle ended up crumpled against the power pole that stood in the front paddock of Jenny's house.

There had been injuries, some serious — broken femurs, basal skull fractures, ruptured organs — but no deaths. Not yet.

Jenny had unearthed the shell of her daughter's long-dead pet from its resting place in the garden and laid it down in the strawberry patch across the road. *That will finish things*, she thought.

For the next year everything was quiet. Then another stunned driver came to her door, and Jenny knew there would be more.

In the autumn, Jenny liked to sit among the naked strawberry plants and watch the sun dip beneath the hills in the late afternoon.

She stayed away from the corner where she'd placed the tortoise shell, particularly if there was a breeze. There, tethered and drooping, the strawberry plants sounded as if they were whispering.

'A life for a life.'

She heard it sometimes when the wind kicked up. Those words, and not the autumn cool, made Jenny shiver.

'A life for a life.'

An abridged taxonomy of little-known ghosts:
A to L

Agraphorum imago The ghost of unfinished stories. A character 31
whose tale never reached the end of the first draft can linger for
decades after the writer has forgotten it. Only the destruction
of the story, or the death of the author, can end the quest for
narrative closure.

Amoris non mutui imago The ghost of an unrequited crush.
Appears wherever two people meet after one is no longer
attracted to the other. This ghost can cause intense humiliation
— or simply wistful lament.

Arbuscularum umbra The ghost of trees felled before their time.
It makes leaves rustle on still nights, and casts scents which
throw people back to their childhoods.

Curriculorum non cursorum imago The ghost of roads not taken.
Even if the ultimate destination is the same, this ghost has an
intense power to instil regret in the most sceptical mind.

Iuventae larva The ghost of the person you once were. This
is a hard spirit, by turns teasing the host with the beauty
and confidence of bygone youth, then haunting them with
reminders of past actions and beliefs that now cause the
deepest shame.

Larvarum fabularum imago The ghost of forgotten ghost stories.
This spirit, whose fables have been lost from the oral tradition,
lurks in the shadows around campfires. It is a propitious
little thing, often jumping in at pauses, hoping to inspire
spontaneous regeneration.

Literariarum personarum umbra The ghost of book characters.
Rare, since they can generally be reincarnated by re-reading
the book. Those that do survive have profound effects on
sensitive readers. May cause pastiche, homage, satire, and
fanfiction.

Locutorum non imago The ghost of words which arrive too late on the tongue. Also known as *Le spectre d'escalier*. This ghost in particular outstays its welcome; the most reliable method of exorcism is writing.

I don't believe any of the conspiracy theories espoused in the videos
I watch on YouTube. I've seen hours of shaky footage where people
argue the moon landing was faked, 9/11 was an inside job, fluoride is
added to water as a form of mass mind control, and that gay people
cause earthquakes.

    I watch them because I find them comforting.

    There are people out there with enough faith in their elected
officials that they believe the government is capable of orchestrating
huge, elaborate intrigues and keeping them hidden for decades. It's
kind of touching, when you think about it.

34

Our luck got worse after the bees died. Everyone's did. Three years ago, bees in the valley started dying — maybe from mites or from pesticides. By the following winter, they were gone.

We're like most of the families around here, just normal. The community has its own rituals and stories. Bread and milk for pixies. Only using the left door of the church hall. Why Gold Creek bends that way.

And telling the bees.

Any time something important happens, tell the bees. When I got engaged, the first thing I did was go to the hives and let the bees know I'd said yes. I gave them the news even before I told my parents.

But now the hives are empty, and our luck is getting worse. My daughter was accepted into a summer science camp — but when she went, she was miserable and other kids were mean.

Our neighbour set up a new business, but things went wrong from the start. Supplies came late, contractors disappeared, clients didn't pay what they'd agreed to. All around our little community, important events were hit by bad luck. Homes damaged, relationships soured, babies born sickly.

So, when I heard the design I'd worked on was a finalist for a major public building, I decided to see what I could do.

I walked down to the back field, where the old hive stood, rotting at the base. I knew there were no bees left. But when I approached, the hive wasn't silent — buzzing emanated from its core. It wasn't the happy drone of thousands of workers bringing back pollen. One solitary buzz. Loud.

The queen bee cannot fly. She is still in there, aged and alone and abandoned to her rage.

I left without telling her anything.

On cold nights his home-made radio came on, broadcasting the
screams of those cosmonauts airbrushed out of 1950s photographs.

Spring flowers pop their heads above ground, right on schedule.
'You're in for a shock,' she told them.

'A man can get used to hanging if he hangs long enough.'
'Then what happens?'
'Depends if he can stand the monotony.'

Farmers who used shotguns to scare birds from their crops found
that the problem got worse. 'Pellet Dodging' became a rite of passage
for adolescent corvids.

He spoke in two ways: profound and meaningless. Often with the
same words.

It takes an inexperienced nurse blowing out one of his veins for Noah to understand what 'chronic' means.

He'd been so proud of his veins when he was first diagnosed. They held up through blood tests, infusions, and the initial hospital stays.

But this time the nurse doesn't tell Noah how good his veins are. Instead she mentions the scarring in the crook of his elbow from all the injections. Then she tries going in, screws it up, and delivers half a phial of liquid fire into Noah's arm.

His skin reddens, hives bubble toward his armpit. The doctor arrives, kicks out his mates, and Noah realises this will keep happening.

He knew he was sick. He'd been tired and sore, and nothing helped. Noah consulted Dr Google — both before and after the specialist appointment — and knew it wasn't something you just got over.

But it was still more funny than tragic when the smell of a sausage sizzle made him chunder in the Bunnings carpark. Hospital stays were just boring. Missing rugby season hurt less than he'd expected, given he'd been getting pummelled. Noah could handle it.

It didn't sink in until his best asset (medically speaking) had failed him, that things would never go back to the way they were. He wouldn't play rugby next season, might never play again.

Drunken shenanigans with the boys wouldn't be the same, if he was even allowed to drink in the future. Opportunistic infections, appointments, pills to combat the side effects of other pills ... Those weren't going away. Noah would get better this time, but he was never going to get *better*.

After things settle, Noah's mum texts him.

I'm on the way ♥ *Need anything?*

Noah wipes his eyes with his hospital gown before replying.

Nah, I'm fine.

Windfall

Every year, my sister played her ace — '*You* have to pick up the apples Jonathan, it's *your* tree.'

It wasn't my tree. Our grandparents had planted Jonathans after my uncle Jonny died, as my sister well knew. But still, the tree and I had some affinity, so I picked up the apples.

Collecting windfall apples was the worst Easter chore. At our bach we had a peach tree that blossomed but never fruited, and the apple tree, which produced more fruit than we could eat.

What I loathed wasn't the stinking sliminess of putting my thumb through a rotten apple, nor the codling caterpillars squirming inside my collar — though both were awful. What I hated most were the wasps.

Bees are reasonable creatures. Stay still, the bee decides you aren't a flower, and off it flies. I imagine it apologises for short-sightedness as it goes.

Wasps, however, do not listen to reason. They just want to watch the world burn. Wasps are vicious towards small boys who are trying to come between them and a massive haul of sugary windfall apples.

Every buzz was a potential bastard creature, poised to sting me 18 times just because it could. Even picking good apples from the upper branches was fraught, because then a wasp was in position to sting me in the face.

I probably didn't get stung more than three times. But the memory was enough that when my wife suggested planting an apple tree in the garden, I vetoed the idea in favour of early-season peaches. We've been waiting four years for the first peach, but it's still worth it.

You know what I can appreciate? Falling in love with bastards. You know where you stand with them.

So, bastards, fine. It's when you fall for sweethearts — that's what screws you up.

I'd say it was the peanut butter pie that did it, except my idiot self was in love with him months before that.

Love. Limerence. Felt the same.

Fucker ruined peanut butter pie for me either way.

It was half-melted when he offered it to me in a crumpled Burger King bag. He had the gall to look apologetic, to give me a little smile that showed his chipped front tooth, and ask me if he'd remembered right — was it my favourite?

Of course he'd bloody remembered right.

There are some crushes that are enjoyable. That bring a frisson of excitement to an otherwise dull day.

This was not one of those crushes.

This was one of those crushes that destroys you. Because he'll never be interested, but he's so goddamned kind and thoughtful he ruins you for any other man. As well as your favourite pudding.

With a bastard I could have appealed to his libido and felt reasonably safe. Instead I wormed in next to him at every opportunity, puppy-eyed and hopeless, unsure if he didn't notice, or just pretended not to.

I mean, I was not subtle.

By the end of winter, enough was enough. I went cold turkey, banished myself from his presence, gave up Burger King, and had meaningless sex in the hope it would make him mean less to me.

Perhaps it worked. I don't think of him as often. But the briefest taste can take me back — in love, chest tight. Suffocated by that memory of the closest I got: proof that he once thought of me while I wasn't around.

After a certain point the difference
between one and infinity becomes
academic

I am looking at a painting. It is hyper realistic, with details so fine a casual glance might suggest it is a photograph, but when I inspect the work closer, I can see delicate brush strokes in the tempera.

The painting depicts a garden in the first bud of spring, and seen from the back, an artist working on a painting. The artist wears a hat which obscures most of his head, and the hat bears creases where it was stored over winter.

The artist's canvas takes up much of the space in the painting. However, instead of depicting the garden in bud, that canvas bursts with trees in autumn colours: leaves red and gold, trunks touched with shadow.

Amongst this, there is another artist working on a painting. It could be the same artist: both are slender and both wear hats, but from the back it is impossible to tell.

The autumn artist depicts the full bloom of summer, verdant and green. And there is another artist, this time shaded by a small umbrella, the blue of it faded and insubstantial against the riot of colour around him.

I peer closer, trying to see which season the summer artist is painting, to recognise the garden in the future, or the past — but his canvas is too small now to properly make out. The fine details can only impart the fact that the summer artist is painting yet another artist, who is painting another, and another.

I squint, sure I will be able to see it if I focus, and pull my woollen hat further down over my ears to block out the chill.

I am looking at a painting.

Tina Chaibi, Guest Writer.

You will likely have heard the buzzword 'climate dissonance' in the media, relating to the peculiar state of unhappiness that results from understanding climate change.

Unfortunately, this phrase is not well-used by most outlets. It has become a shorthand for standard cognitive dissonance that is expressed in a way influenced by global warming. A typical example is the dissonance between the desire to believe one is environmentally conscious, and the desire to travel by aeroplane.

True climate dissonance is more subtle and intriguing. A localised feeling of happiness due to weather phenomena — such as a warm autumn day — clashes with a larger unease as the individual remembers what warm autumns mean for the global climate. This clash produces distress greater than the feeling of unease alone.

What makes climate dissonance both interesting and frustrating is the difficulty in resolving the dissonant state. An individual experiencing climate dissonance cannot forget the perilous state of the environment. At the same time, forcing oneself to cease enjoying pleasant surroundings is close to impossible.

Only when the local environment has degraded to the extent that the experience is no longer enjoyable does climate dissonance abate. It is hard to enjoy a hot day during a severe drought.

The number of individuals who experience climate dissonance is increasing as extreme weather events become more common, and these events turn former global warming deniers into grudging believers. This lends itself to a broader hypothesis that climate dissonance is yet to peak in the general population.

Unfortunately, by the time climate dissonance does peak, the global environment will have been battered by superstorms, scoured by drought, and coastal cities will only be accessible by boat.

Climate dissonance will then quickly cease in everyone who experiences it, one way or the other.

Kia Ora Students,

University administration has noticed higher-than-normal numbers of time travellers appearing this semester.

The Vice-Chancellor's Office would like to take this opportunity to reassure students that Everything is Fine.

The Head of Department for Physics, Dr Amanda Wu, is keeping us informed about the implications of time travel. She warns that students should not approach any time-travel device that appears on campus. Disrupting these could maroon our visitors from the future or cause a universe-ending paradox. We want to assure students that a universe-ending time paradox is very unlikely, but in the interest of openness and transparency, you should note the possibility.

Some students have asked time travellers for information about their upcoming exams. This is a breach of your Academic Integrity Policy, and anyone using information gleaned from the future to gain an unfair advantage may be subject to disciplinary processes.

We are not being complacent about the possible consequences of rogue time travellers. Sanitiser stations are available around campus, and we encourage you to use them if you feel anxious about super-bacteria from the future to which your immune system has no defence.

Sadly, it has also come to our attention that a small number of individuals have spread rumours that the time travellers visit the Music Department because one or more music students will commit horrific acts of genocide in the future. These rumours are hurtful and go against our university's commitment to fostering an inclusive community. *He waka eke noa.* #BeKind

If you are worried about paradoxes, super-bacteria, deadly futuristic weaponry, or the possibility you will be subjugated by a brutal dictatorship originating from a cabal of musicians at this university, the student counselling service is always available to you.

Yours sincerely,
    Professor R. Serling
    Vice-Chancellor

Wednesday

46   On Wednesday, I realised I had three new bones in my body. I made a 'Found' post on Facebook, though I wasn't sure how I'd return the bones if anyone claimed them.

The email hits my inbox with a big red flag.
... It is incumbent upon everyone to ensure we properly exercise our responsibilities to our shareholders.

There is a roundtable meeting to discuss how our company can best profit from disaster. The term 'roundtable' is a misnomer, since the 13 participants don't get around a table any more. We use Zoom.

We're Marketing and have nothing to add: no one needs clever marketing to sell a drug that will save you from the apocalypse. Instead, we listen to financiers, and doctors discuss prices for individuals, insurance companies, governments. What the market will bear. How fast manufacturing can be scaled.

This is normal.

Then the Assistant CFO from a shell corporation that owns nothing but patents taps his microphone.

'Could our business plan benefit from, say, manufacturing at seventy-five percent capacity for the next three months?'

The silence which follows has weight, while the ACFO steeples his fingers.

Manufacturing responds first. 'That would result in supply shortages. Significant supply shortages.'

'But higher price points for the duration?' The question isn't genuine — the ACFO is not stupid. He is focused, and he is cunning.

Medical cuts in. 'The loss rate will be higher than acceptable.'

'We could adjust the ALR to maximise PPU.' The ACFO speaks in acronyms, distancing himself from meaning, removing the human element of words. We have reached the true crux of the meeting.

Discussion is conducted. ALR is adjusted. Output is set at 80 percent. Projected PPU is increased by seven percent. Total projected additional profit: $7.6 billion. We start drafting press releases about overcoming the challenges of mass-scaling production.

The ACFO is the first to leave the call, and Zoom chimes. One by one others do the same — the app chimes with every exit, tolling like a bell.

48

We invited robots into every part of our lives, but drew the line at inviting them into our deaths.

It would have been a most natural place to intervene — a bot would not need high-level automation to go through the steps of routine embalming, and the corpse wouldn't notice.

But relatives reacted with horror. There was something ghoulish in the idea of handing their dearly departed over to machines, even if it was cheaper.

Several major religions prohibited the practice outright. Some smaller sects encouraged it, since it removed unclean work from human hands.

Most of the crematoria that went 'full AI' had government contracts to process unclaimed bodies. They were dubbed 'Potters' Parlours'.

Funeral homes advertised that they employed real, empathetic human beings to prepare the deceased for their final viewings. Morticians found their wages remained stagnant, even as their services were at a premium.

The phenomenon was a particular boon to academics. Social psychologists posited that as time passed and AI became ubiquitous, opposition would cease. Theologians debated the future implications for religious burials. Historians and anthropologists discussed death rites across time and culture — always mentioning the customs of Ancient Egypt somewhere.

A decade after robotic embalming became widely available — with little sign either that we were becoming less averse to the idea, or less fascinated by our own aversion — it began to feature in comedy routines. One joke suggested the resistance was engineered to give PhD students something to research.

Within a year such jokes were déclassé, relegated to the comedy dead zone of airline food and ex-wives.

An object lesson in why you should
always read the terms and conditions
before clicking accept

He's sweating. That's nothing new — they always sweat. He looks
up, fear naked on his face, so I smile beatifically.
  'Take your time. I understand, it's a dense document.'
  His eyes flick down to the papers. 'R-r-really?'
  'Absolutely. As much as you need.'
  His breath eases and he returns to reading.
  'Do you mind if I step out?' He flinches when I speak. 'Devil
makes work for idle hands and all that.'
  'That's, uh, fine,' he says.
  'Appreciated.'
  The door clicks shut behind me. It's a perfect system —
condemned souls spend a hellish eternity poring over the contract,
looking for loopholes.

The presenter wore a boy-band microphone, jeans with designer holes in them, and too much hair gel. 'We're talking about a breakthrough in our understanding of the human brain!' he enthused.

'And using it to sell people shit,' I muttered.

It wasn't a breakthrough. I'd studied psychology at undergrad and learned the basics about neural pathways through higher and lower cortices. The presenter was jizzing over pathway-specific advertising.

Interesting stuff, and my boss was paying me to be here. But it all seemed odd. The parts of the brain we could target didn't go through intellectual reasoning. This would short-circuit peoples' ability to filter messages, to discern.

I paid more attention to the practicalities — layering messages to appeal to lower-order pathways, integrating both visual and audio processes. Though I was in the back row, huge screens ensured I caught the presenter's every gesture, and since the sound was cranked to Michael Bay levels, there was no chance of zoning out.

I'd always been fascinated by the brain, though I wasn't smart enough to study neurology. Change the brain, and you change the experience of the universe. I found myself nodding as the presenter talked about altering the message to alter the brain.

There was something about the ability to engender goodwill through unrelated messaging that made me pleased I could get a peek behind the curtain.

In the Q&A someone asked about ethics, ads targeted at children, ads that could contribute to social ills. Another asked whether the technology could be used to manipulate elections, but I didn't listen to the answers.

At the end of the discussion, I lined up and shook hands with the presenter. I thanked him for educating me on such a ground-breaking tool, trying to mimic his charming smile.

I queued for 45 minutes, but the supermarket had no flour. I snapped a picture of the shelves for Twitter — *Where's all the flour gone? I gotta stress bake.*

A flurry of retweets indicated I wasn't alone.

Then I got a message, a stranger sliding into my DMs, no preamble:

I know a guy.

You know a guy?

He's got flour.

I wanted details. He didn't *know* the guy, but he knew a guy who knew the guy. I promised fresh-baked ginger slice all along the chain, until I found myself with a stranger at a Four Square, ten minutes after closing. We didn't shake hands.

It was a 30 kg bag of flour. 'I was going to divide it up,' said my supplier, 'Only ...'

Only he'd gotten nervous. He could have made a lot from Glad bags of flour. But the guy sold milk and overpriced lollies — he wasn't cut out for this kind of life.

My social feeds were full of bakers jonesing for the good stuff. I could sift through them for buyers.

I took the flour. And the Glad bags. I covered them up in the back of my car and drove home practising excuses. 'Just going to the supermarket, Officer.'

Flour dealing was a three-man job; my flatmates siphoning premium white into bags while I spread the word on messaging apps and in secret groups. I'd sold it all before they'd parcelled it out.

We delivered on foot, stretching the limits of 'local', backpacks full, faces masked. Made drops in letter boxes and on doorsteps, online payment only, no contact.

After two days, all I had left was a full flour bin, and ginger crunch awaiting pickup.

But the messages kept coming. So I started looking again, for another guy who knew a guy.

'In one dimension, your worst fear will never occur. In another, it's
already happened.'
'Which is safer?'
'The second.'

The impetus to change was clear: the destruction of our species.
The aliens watched with pity as we failed, then they hit the button.

Robots taking our jobs was a given. Office fridges leaving notes even
more passive-aggressive than ours — that was a surprise.

I wasn't sure which was worse: trackers beaming ads into our
REM sleep, or when copyright notices arrived for the contents of
our dreams.

While the breakfast trolley rattles down the corridor, Jeremy waits. He moves to the window as the nurse wakes Gail, takes her blood pressure, passes over medication.

After breakfast, Jeremy folds himself up at the end of Gail's bed and watches her fall into a doze.

Gail's husband Harold arrives mid-morning, bringing the paper. He tells Gail that no visitors are scheduled until tomorrow. Together they complete the crossword — a task which takes longer every day.

In the afternoon the doctor makes his rounds, giving Gail the news that there is no news. After a few minutes of chat, the young doctor looks awkward and brings out a book for Gail to autograph. A tremor distorts her signature.

It's been 30 years since Gail wrote this book, and she strokes the cover gently. The art is similar to the original printing, but it's a new edition. Newish, anyway. A sort-of souvenir, from a life long gone.

The doctor leaves for his next patient, and Gail closes her eyes. Just when she might have drifted off, she turns to Harold.

'I worry ...'

Harold takes her hand. 'Worry about what?'

'Whether I've told enough stories. All those notebooks ...'

Jeremy looks up. He lives somewhere in a first draft, scrawled in a mildewed notebook, unfinished for 50 years.

Harold smiles at his wife and squeezes her hand a little. 'You've told them all, love.'

Jeremy's throat is so tight he can only shake his head.

With her fingers in Harold's, Gail relaxes against her pillow, and falls asleep.

In the depths of night, Jeremy waits. He watches over Gail, sleeping in the hospice half-light, willing her to keep breathing.

'Stop picking.'   55

My nails, cut so short that the tips of my fingers are red-raw,
cease trying to lift away the scabbing on the inside of my elbow.
I know Mother is waiting for me to say it itches, so I keep quiet.

It doesn't itch, not really. Instead, it is a tightness; my skin feels
as if there is something underneath, trying to get out.

The lake is cold at this time of year. It is deep, but very clear — in
the right light I can see glimmers of silver, just at the point where
the water becomes too dark to clearly make out a sinking stone.

I keep trying to touch the bottom, but I haven't been able to
yet. I think I am getting closer, though it is hard to know, with
nothing other than a watch on the jetty to tell me how long I can
hold my breath.

Mother wishes I would stop swimming, because afterwards my
skin gets even worse. Huge flakes slough away, revealing flesh that is
smooth and firm. The cracks disclose a skin which is not really skin
— too grey and too cold and too sleek.

After I come back from the lake she slathers on moisturiser, but
it doesn't do anything other than prolong the process. Then she tells
me to stop picking while the top layer of my skin gets tighter and
tighter. It falls off anyway, whether I pick or don't.

I don't care about that. I love the water. I am certain I will reach
the bottom of the lake soon, and there, no one has skin.

I arrived home from work to find Fionn sitting on a paint-spattered bedsheet, a complex arrangement of copper wire, fairy lights, and tiny glass bottles around him.

'What're you doing?'

He held a bundle of smouldering sage, passing it over the assembled objects.

'Magic.'

Fionn was a designer and artist. That he'd decided to add 'Witch' to his CV didn't surprise me.

'You're going to set off the smoke alarm.'

His lopsided smile pressed a dimple into his left cheek. I bent down to kiss him, wincing at the smell of burning herbs.

'No,' he said, 'I'm going to make a light to shine bright and bring positive energy.'

'Will it work?'

'We'll see.'

Watching Fionn turn the objects into a swirl of lights that painted the walls with dancing copper shards and turned his sandy hair gold — that was magic enough for me.

After the assault, Fionn was scared of the dark. We moved closer to his parents, and the bottle-light sculpture went into storage. The brain damage affected his motor skills, and art became a reminder of what he'd lost.

It was months before he'd even be alone at night, so when I was at an office party and learned the power was out for half my suburb, I raced home. Fionn might have forgotten where the torch was, and if he panicked he might not be able to unlock his phone.

Our flat was dark. I groped my way up the stairs, calling 'Fionn?'

Silence.

Then I saw it. Along the corridor to our bedroom, the merest flash. I opened the door to find Fionn asleep, shards of copper light dancing across the walls and ceiling, turning his sandy hair to gold.

Hephaestus

At night he dreams of a giant, an anvil, a forge. The hot orange light
illuminates a look of wonder as the colossus hammers Adam into birth.

Then, when he goes into work, Hef can't produce anything even close.
The man in his dreams works with nothing more than iron and steel.
Hef works with carbon fibre and silicon, encasing platinum, silver and
rare earth metals, but the product lacks the beauty of its components.

    Hef's robot doesn't look human — isn't even supposed to look
human, since it must avoid the uncanny valley. The technology isn't
there anyway. Its feet are flat panels with one articulated big toe,
because the gyroscopic balancing system cannot compensate for
an arch.

    The robot's utilitarian design extends upwards. Its short frame
is squat and wide for strength and stability. Its limbs are cubes and
rectangles attached to spherical joints. There is no hint of the graceful
curves which make up the human body.

    In his weaker moments, Hef allows himself to imagine. In his mind
he is holding a perfect android, cradling it like a small child. Its body is
not a square of dull matte grey, but a filigree of titanium and gold, one
moment inanimate, the next — alive.

Hef stands behind his company's CEO while the programmers
demonstrate their robot. He is embarrassed by the machine's clumsy,
halting movements, its inarticulate speech. Yet the reporters are
amazed.

    'We're not trying to replace human beings,' says the CEO, smiling for
the camera. 'After all, if we want more people, we can just create them
the old-fashioned way!'

    Hef doesn't join the scattered laughter. Instead he looks away, looks
inward, feels the illusory wash of heat, and the imaginary weight of the
hammer in his hand.

58

'You had to know it was a terrible idea.'

'I did not. Everyone said I should diversify my income streams!'

'You're a freelance journo! They meant starting a podcast, not ... that.'

'There are ten million podcasts. This was unique. A *true* disruptive enterprise.'

'But did you earn anything?'

'Each crossing was low-profit, sure, but it's tax-free. And I had no setup costs — my cousin wasn't using the kayak. Though he did say he wanted it back.'

'Well, you're going to struggle there, aren't you?'

'That wasn't my fault! How could I know the ferryman would be so touchy?'

'He makes people who can't pay the fare wander the riverbank for eternity! Even you can't be dumb enough to think he'd welcome the competition.'

'I guessed he'd be pissy, but come on. He's got a boat. He could outdo me on service — sweets, bottles of water — even if I did undercut him on price. And he's on the calmest part of the river.'

'How did you get customers?'

'Some people forgot inflation. Some didn't have real silver. But mostly, people find him creepy. You won't get five stars with creepy.'

'Let me get this straight. To reach the afterlife they'd rather cross the river Styx in a two-person kayak with *you* than deal with creepy?'

'Yeah.'

'Wow. All right, hit me — what's your punishment?'

'Well, Charon got Hades to smite my kayak —'

'— your cousin's kayak.'

'My cousin's kayak. But then instead of smiting me, they sent me back here.'

'They let you go.'

'Yeah. Told me I'll discover my punishment next time I'm at the riverbank.'

'Nice. Something to fret over for your remaining years.'

'Tell me about it. I kind of hope I'll die tomorrow, just to give them less time to think up something really disruptive.'

It was life-changing, the day her brother almost drowned.

Not just because of the sudden, terrible presence of mortality in their midst — but because she had saved him. Hauled his lifeless, floppy body from the pool and performed CPR, while their cousin called an ambulance.

He wasn't breathing. She started humming 'Stayin' Alive' to time the compressions, like she'd read on Facebook. By the time the paramedics arrived, he was conscious, with only a concussion from falling and hitting his head.

That day, she decided she wanted to become one of those paramedics.

Except she couldn't pass the first-aid course. Twice she had been too weak to do compressions on the dummy to the right depth for long enough.

She couldn't understand it — her brother was 18, well-built, and she'd resuscitated him easily enough. She supposed it had been adrenaline.

Then came a second accident. The little boy from across the street, rushing into the road. The car, going too fast to stop. A screech, a thud, and her neighbour hit the ground like a broken toy.

'Doctors ABCD ... Doctors ABCD ...,' she muttered, trying to find a pulse. She couldn't. She checked his airway, mindful of spinal trauma. Then, there it was! A fluttering in his neck, where 30 seconds ago there was nothing. Again she met the paramedics, and accompanied her neighbour to the hospital.

She sat on a plastic chair in the waiting room for hours, until the boy's mother emerged, hugged her tight, and sobbed that he was going to be okay.

'I still can't pass that dummy test,' she complained to her brother.

'Maybe you only save people who've actually died,' he said, 'That would explain everything.' They both laughed.

The next morning, she signed up for her third first-aid course.

Part I

After my childhood experiences with the tooth fairy, I proposed the
following exchange to the fair folk. They are free to have all my teeth
— including the four wisdom teeth — so long as the teeth remain
in my head, and they take the rest of me as well. To my ongoing
disappointment, the fae have yet to accept this excellent offer.

Part II
Perhaps if I throw in my femurs?

62

You approach the door. In place of a security guard there is a sphinx. She asks you a riddle. You answer it correctly, but she pretends she cannot hear you.

The receptionist asks for your name. She asks for your client number. She asks for your most painful childhood memory. She asks for a sliver of your soul.

You wait. Your name will be called. Hours pass. Days. Years. When they call your name you no longer recognise it.

In the waiting area you see a man drinking a beer. You see a man drinking a can of Woodstock. You see a man drinking the blood of the damned. He has very clean fingernails.

A poster states 'The only disability is a bad attitude'. A man using a wheelchair touches the poster. Immediately, he levitates out of his chair, then begins to glow with a pulsing white light.

Your case worker asks if you are in a relationship. You start to say no. Before you can, you are suddenly in a relationship. You are the bride of an abomination whose name cannot be uttered by the human mouth.

A bell rings. A column of flame erupts and engulfs the person next to you. The staff applaud in unison.

You sign a form stating you understand your rights. You sign a form stating you understand your responsibilities. You sign a form stating you understand how the universe will destroy itself. And then you do understand. You begin to scream.

Thursday

64   On Thursday, I discovered a note stuck to my fridge with souvenir magnets
       from Europa. The note was a support ticket, claiming I had been in
       contact regarding the current state of the universe:
            *REINSTALLATION WILL OCCUR OVER THE WEEKEND. PLEASE DO
       NOT REPLY TO THIS ADDRESS, AS IT IS UNMONITORED.* The address
       was a series of glyphs.

Monster spray

Morgan thought it was sweet, the way her seven-year-old son Andrew (and here she could almost hear him interject 'seven and three-quarters!') came to her every night before bed and asked her to check for monsters.

She got the idea of 'monster spray' from the internet, and went around Andrew's room spraying inside the cupboard and under the bed with a mixture of water and lavender oil. It meant she had to be vigilant about mould, but Morgan enjoyed playing Warrior Mum — even if she was only armed with a plant mister.

Lying in bed, Andrew waited until the soft burble of his parents talking had given way to the sharper tones of the TV. Then he rolled towards the side of his bed and flopped his torso over the edge. He wriggled forward until he was looking underneath, hair brushing the carpet.

'Hey,' he whispered, 'Hey, Monster.'

Silence.

'Monster, hello?' he said, louder.

The thing under the bed cracked an eye. It had many eyes to choose from.

'Are you okay?' asked Andrew, 'Did you get enough water?'

'Oh yes, plenty,' it replied, in a voice that reminded Andrew of dry sticks snapping, 'Though it would be nice to have rosewater, rather than lavender — just for variety.'

Andrew considered it, 'I'll see if I can get Mum to change it, but I'll have to be crafty about asking.'

After a few more turns and shuffles, Andrew was drifting off to sleep. Eight inches beneath him, the monster stayed awake for some hours afterward.

We have always been here. There are so many lies about autism; I want to say that straight away. We have always been here.

We are not a punishment. Your beautiful child wasn't replaced by a monster because you vaccinated them or smoked while pregnant or didn't feed your kid organic baby food.

Obviously, we aren't monsters. We are still beautiful children, beautiful adults. Most of us. Some of us are bad because in any group of people there will be a subset who are bad. That has nothing to do with being autistic, just to do with being human.

People used to say we were changelings, left by fairies who stole children away in the night.

When I was little I believed that, but I got it the wrong way round, since I found out about the changeling idea just after I started losing my baby teeth. And the tooth fairy had come and taken my disgusting teeth away, and left me money. I got something of value in exchange for something that did not have value.

So for a few years I thought that fairies took neurotypical babies and left autistic ones in the same way. I was a treasure gifted to my parents: someone of true value.

I did eventually sort out my misunderstanding, but for a while it was pretty good because otherwise I would have started feeling bad about myself even earlier.

Dad knocked out a man's tooth once. The man said I should be killed because I had a meltdown in the supermarket. Perhaps that's why the fairies gave me to my particular parents. They knew there would be extra teeth to collect.

'Don't call him an idiot,' she thinks, *'Yell the answer but don't call him an idiot!'*

'It's alliteration, idiot!'

The entire class laughs. Laughs with her, laughs at Ezra, who flushes dark and looks at the floor. And she can't understand why she did it. She didn't want to embarrass him, she was just bored, just wanted to move on.

Her teacher keeps her after class. She likes Miss Wheeler, likes her triple-pierced ears, so the sad look on her face is almost worse than detention.

'Amy,' she says, 'There was no need to call out the way you did.'

'Sorry, Miss.' And she is sorry, she's always sorry, she was sorry even before the words left her mouth — but she still said them anyway.

'You've done that before. I know everyone laughs, but it's not really funny, is it?'

She does it in all her classes, lobs a one-line grenade into the middle of the room and watches the resulting detonation. She happens to think it is pretty funny. What's not funny is the way she can't seem to stop herself, the way she never gets a moment between thinking she could do a thing and doing it.

Miss Wheeler is still staring at her.

'No Miss, I guess not.'

'Try a bit harder to hold it in next time, eh? And apologise to Ezra.'

'Yeah, I will. Sorry again.'

She doesn't apologise, because if she was Ezra, she wouldn't want to hear it. She also doesn't tell Miss Wheeler that she's trying as hard as she can, because that will just sound like a lie next time it happens.

Every school report she's ever had says that: "Must try harder". And she wonders how long it will be before she's finally allowed to give up.

68   Friends say my new neighbourhood is pretty rough, and they might
      have a point. Walking to the bus stop on any given day, I'll see at least
      two pieces of broken furniture sitting on the berm. The neighbours own
      a homicidal Staffordshire Terrier rather than a Labrador. On Friday
      and Saturday nights there's a security guard outside the liquor store.

      However, the two biggest differences I've noticed from the posh
      inner suburbs are: there are a lot more laundromats, and a lot fewer
      giant four-wheel drives. It's a net positive from my point of view. I'm
      now less likely to be hit by a car, and — if it were to happen — more
      likely to be wearing clean underwear.

1. Any arson committed during a riot, though only if done with a Molotov cocktail. You don't want to be the dickhead fidgeting with matches trying to get a shop to catch fire.

2. Your ex's stuff. If they left it at your place, after a month it becomes yours. If you set it on fire before the month is up, they can't get it back anyway.

3. Creepy old houses in the woods. This kind of arson is even encouraged, since it allows the trapped spirits to move on. Check there's not a fire ban beforehand.

4. The body of the foe you vanquished at the climax of your hero's journey. Especially if he repented from evil in the final act. Do not throw yourself on the pyre. No one needs that kind of drama.

5. The crumbling old family bungalow that keeps you trapped in a toxic relationship with your mother. Though not if she is in there at the time. Then it's just murder.

6. Zombies.

7. Copies of *Mein Kampf* or any other Nazi paraphernalia. This may or may not include actual Nazis.

8. Cursed paintings. First, remove the painting from the wall. There's no need to waste a good house. Rent is already too high.

9. The minutiae of your old life, before you reinvent yourself in a new town, city, or country.

10. That abandoned warehouse I burned to the ground, your Honour.

The two strangers in the delivery van are not meant to look in the box. They have received Very Specific Instructions, one of which is Do Not Look In The Box.

Still, there isn't a whole lot stopping Sione from looking in the box. Barely any tape, no polypropylene strapping or plastic wrap. He could easily look, then just as easily bundle it back up again. He wonders if it is a test — though if he passes this test, then what?

De Wet has spent the last hour convinced there is a severed head in the box. When he started driving, that had just been a passing thought, the result of watching *Se7en* too many times. Now it's all he can think about. He doesn't want to know what *is* in the box — he only wants to know that it's not a severed head.

When they'd started driving, the two men had tried to make conversation, but they had little in common. Sione had a lot of family, but De Wet had almost none. De Wet followed cricket while Sione played league, and there was only so long they could talk about superhero movies.

Anthrax? Diamonds? A curse? Nothing at all? A dozen times Sione is about to ask De Wet what he thinks it is, but decides not to. If they start discussing it, the temptation to look might overwhelm them.

It is, perhaps, the only thing the two men actually share: neither will ever know what the other thinks they are transporting.

For decades afterwards, De Wet and Sione will occasionally think of one another, appearing in sudden bursts of memory, united in not knowing.

But when have we ever just left
well enough alone?

Thank you for contacting LivingHistoryInc (LHI), the Number One service for all you could ever want to know about your exciting* past life!

Before we begin, LHI has been asked by the [INSERT RELEVANT REGULATORY BODY] to present the following information:

- It is impossible to have been someone in a past life if that person did not die prior to your birth.

- Fictional characters cannot be reborn as real people.

- Much of the historical population worked in agriculture, and thus most currently living persons will not have been famous in a past life.

Furthermore, LHI would like to remind clients of the following:

- All payments are made upfront and in full. No refund is available if you are unhappy about who you were in a past life.

- Should you not wish to know if you were evil in your past life, please affirm below. No refunds will be provided in this instance.

- The *Contact Your Past Self!* package is only available if your previous incarnation was literate in English.

- Despite any feelings that you must have been Marilyn Monroe, William Shakespeare, or any other famous historical figure, LHI cannot promise to affirm assumptions of this nature.

- LHI accepts no responsibility for any damages caused by the discovery of historical grievances between any currently living persons or groups.

• •

We at LHI are eager to help you uncover the mysteries of your past! Our process is scientifically proven, easy, and has very few side effects![†]

Find out who you were Yesterday, Today!™

* LHI accepts no responsibility for the relative excitement of past lives.

† Side effects include anal leakage, searing pain, nausea, dizziness, headaches, and temporary or permanent loss of vision. Please consult your health professional should you experience any or all of these effects.

'Why must the worlds in my dreams be destroyed when I wake up?'
'Why do you think we stop existing because you're not watching?'
She felt relief go through her, just before her alarm rang.

I pour drinks for returned space travellers while they try to accept the
home they dreamed of was not a place, but a time.

The apprentice eyed the InSinkErator carefully. She suspected it was
just pretending to be tame. It had bitten its master's hand already.

The warehouse was neatly arranged. Ancient horrors, dimensionless
beasts, the terrors of alternate timelines. A pity there was no map.

Empathy generators worked on most people, but not all. We voted the
outliers into power anyway. Probably because we felt sorry for them.

'Pity we don't have a sample of her DNA,' one of the research team joked, looking at the Mona Lisa. 'Then we could say for certain.'

We had Leonardo's DNA. He'd written letters, constructed models, created art. It took tens of thousands of samples and eliminations, but we were finally able to reconstruct the great man's genome. When the rendering of his face appeared, we popped the champagne.

There are no secrets any more. They no longer serve us. For far too long mind-state analysis was crude — smile if happy, frown if sad — and too easily faked. Now, with DNA sequencing, phenotype projection, population analysis, age/weight alterations, and the dozen other metrics which are computed in seconds, anyone can read thoughts from facial expressions.

When we're performing historical readings on paintings or photographs that took more than an instant to capture, it gets muddy — but the broad strokes are there. We have extensive databases to discern health status, sexual orientation, region of birth, nutrition levels, and more. State of mind is more difficult, but we can make some very educated guesses.

There have been protests. Discussion of a 'right' to secrecy. A 'right' to private thought. Even protests about using the technology on long-dead subjects, as though they had any need for privacy now.

But that was a distraction. We took the chance to rediscover history; to know, rather than to guess. Rights took a back seat to opportunities.

And Lisa? We can't be sure, but we think she smiled because she was sleeping with the painter.

There's a weird smell in here — more than just the old blue-grey institutional carpet. And I'm sure I've been around this corner before.

Some places exist half a dimension away. Major airports, unfamiliar houses at night, empty construction sites. They are malleable, bigger than they look, and constantly changing. But I never expected to find a soft place in the middle of my university.

It's ridiculous; this is the Arts Building, not Daedalus' labyrinth. I've been to my supervisor's office before. I just can't find it now.

I tried the floor above where I thought it was, then the floor below, just in case. Now I'm wandering, ten minutes late, hoping to stumble across it. I found the same exit twice without doubling back, but since then I haven't seen any.

My 'rational' brain is telling me that's progress. My 'overdramatic bitch' brain is convinced the exits no longer exist.

One shoelace flaps loose, but I don't stop to tie it. Strange noises echo behind me. I tell myself it's only the 'clunk' that comes from poorly maintained photocopiers, but I can't remember seeing a print room on this floor.

I text my supervisor to say I won't make it. I'm too late by now anyway.

The message won't send. It hovers on my screen, the three dots getting my hopes up, before showing a red exclamation mark.

I need to get out of here. Sweat prickles under my arms and trickles down my spine, pooling under my backpack.

The smell is intensifying, rankness of hot breath and the stench of meat.

Was that a snort?

Rounding another corner, I hit a dead end. My chest heaves, pulse thuds in my temples.

I squeeze my eyes shut, trying to find the courage to turn around, and prepare myself to run.

The dare

He went to Poland on a dare, he said, laughing. He'd been eight pints in and using his passport for ID.

'Never use your passport for ID, mate,' he advised. I nodded, though I've never owned a passport.

It was all a big joke, a random cheap flight, most people would end up in Ibiza, he said, but instead he landed in Krakow. He slept in the arrivals hall until the *Policja* moved him on, pointed him in the direction of the nearest pub, just another drunk Englishman.

'How long did you stay?' I asked, wondering when this story would turn, when this happy-go-lucky booze hound had run into history.

'Five days, I think.'

'You think?'

He shrugged.

He'd been drunk the whole time, he said, slept in hostels with gap-year kids and one night on the floor of a woman who'd kicked him out of bed once they'd finished fucking.

The jaunt had cost a bit, though less than if he'd spent five days drinking in England.

'They like their cheap booze, the Poles,' he confided. 'Love it, brilliant place.'

He'd finished his week-long bender, then flown home, still hammered. Only took one picture, in the departure lounge, just to prove he'd been.

'You didn't go anywhere else?' I asked, 'Didn't go see the camps, or what's left of them?'

He looked baffled and shook his head. 'Why would I want to do that? Sounds bloody morbid if you ask me.'

'So, what did you win?' I said, and took a drink. 'For the dare?'

His good cheer disappeared with the last of his pint. He looked at me like I'd let him down. 'That wasn't the point, mate,' he said, voice grave. 'That was never the point.'

76

It started with tea. Cups of it, going cold on the desk beside Ipsi's computer. He brewed his tea strong and black, then left it overnight — etching the insides of the team's communal mugs with dark stains.

'Do you ever actually drink tea?' I asked, trying to scrub out the offending crockery. 'Or do you just make it for fun?'

'It's an offering,' he replied, as though that was obvious. 'Did you know that in Taiwan, programmers leave snacks next to their computers to help their code compile?'

'We're not in Taiwan,' I said. 'You're not Taiwanese.'

'The principle still holds.'

Before I could ask what principle, Ipsi left the kitchenette, mug of tea in hand.

He moved on to snacks two months later, at the tail end of a chaotic sprint. It wasn't much: a handful of Skittles or gummy bears sitting on his workstation where the rest of us kept toys and sticky notes.

But it seemed to work. Ipsi's debugging took less time; his code had fewer syntax issues.

The week before launch I worked until the small hours, trying to catch errant parentheses. The third night, dizzy with exhaustion, I bought two packets of wine gums from the vending machine. I arranged them around my keyboard in neat groups, sorted by colour. Then I fell asleep on my desk.

I awoke to Ipsi waving a coffee under my nose.

'I see you've come around to my way of thinking,' he said, while I gulped espresso. I nodded. It wasn't until I'd finished my coffee that I noticed all the red wine gums were gone.

'Doesn't hurt to make offerings to local gods,' said Ipsi. 'You never know who might be hungry.'

Friday

78

On Friday, I arrived at work to find there was a party at my office. My co-workers and I socialised from 8:30 to 4:30, then we all sat down for after-drinks work. I got as much work done as I had the previous Friday.

Boat people

We knew it would be necessary to keep some people conscious on the ship. We needed a crew, and the length of our potential journey meant we would have to replace that crew when they reached retirement age.

We had to keep certain skills alive — the skills needed to pilot the ship, and to prosper once we reached our destination.

And people are social creatures. We couldn't condemn our crew to lifetimes of loneliness. We understood the decision meant some children born in space would not experience life outside the ship, but we reasoned they could not miss what they never knew.

Across the galaxy we carried a small town of waking occupants, a small city of humans in cryosleep, and the makings of a small country in sperm, eggs, and embryos.

Humans in space are still humans. And facing the ultimate adversity — the death throes of our planet — plenty of people turned to gallows humour.

Within a month — a unit of time which no longer held any real meaning — the more scurrilous travellers had started calling us 'boat people'. We imagined landing on an already-populated planet, seeking asylum in a language the inhabitants didn't understand, and with all the materials to be fruitful and multiply. So, we gave ourselves an ironic name: The Influx.

Irony never lasts. By the third generation after Earth, *influxian* was the standard collective noun for the occupants of our ship. And we almost entirely forgot that 'boat people' was once a pejorative, a term to describe human beings whom our former civilisations had condemned to death because they came from the wrong piece of rock.

Time resists change, that much we knew.

No matter the scale of the aberration time travellers seek to cause, the universe prevents it. A sociopath who went back in time to kill the child Hitler found his gun first jammed, then exploded — taking most of his forearm with it. And the partygoers we sent to Stephen Hawking's 'Time Travellers Meeting' couldn't find the address.

In this, history has proved more resilient to paradox than we ever suspected. You cannot go back in time and murder your grandfather, because once you have been born, circumstance will prevent it.

We now understand that time has always included the interventions of time travellers. There is no 'original' timeline to split and become a 'new' timeline. If time accepts the chronovoyager's acts, then that chronovoyager is now part of the past. Time will protect their actions, just as it protects the actions of someone in their proper time.

However, once we perfected time travel to the point where we could send people forward as well as back, we made a devastating discovery.

This resistance to change also affects the future. If a chronovoyager sees the future actions of a specific person, that person will invariably perform those actions. Even with prior warning, the universe ensures it.

Which means free will, as traditionally understood, does not exist.

When this was publicised, we faced the question of whether it would have been better not to have invented time travel. This would have allowed humanity to continue believing we have free will. And to that question, we have no answer.

Because no matter what we may feel, it was inevitable. We were always going to invent time travel, so we always did.

Where are they now?

The girl in your class who was amazing at art when she was eight now works for a government department. She draws pictures on napkins of the barista making her coffee while she waits for her latte. She always throws the doodles away, even though they are good.

The teenager behind the counter at the ice-cream place where you used to stop during road trips is still there. She tells people she doesn't mind never going anywhere. But after her fourth glass of cheap chardonnay she will admit she still plans her own dream road trip.

The boy who was an arsehole to you all through secondary school is doing well at a finance company and has a good-looking family. Remember, the devil protects his own.

That guy you hit it off with one night and always meant to meet again — except you could never find a time that worked — is now married. He doesn't know it, but he would have been happier married to you. You would not have been happier.

The kid you still feel guilty for bullying lives a nice life. They have a decent career, fulfilling hobbies, and a large circle of family and friends. They don't remember anything about you.

The celebrity you had a crush on is now nowhere. You think you recall their name, but you're wrong. It's the other one.

The thing without a name that has haunted you, the thing you stopped telling people about because they dismissed it as just your imagination ... was never your imagination. It's right behind you.

Moli hated it when people asked what he did for a job. He struggled to put it in a good light. The broad answer was he worked on programming for self-driving cars.

That got people interested. Then they asked more questions and Moli found it awkward to say his job involved programming criteria under which — in the case of a serious accident — a self-driving car would prioritise the lives of its passengers, occupants of other vehicles, or people outside the car.

In his work he had to compromise between someone who broke the law by not wearing a seatbelt and the increased survival rate of someone who had buckled up.

He had spent four months trying to teach a computer to recognise the size of a child. Eight more trialling calculations to assign points to the number of adults worth the life of a toddler.

Moli knew self-driving cars would reduce fatal accidents to almost zero. Knew the most dangerous time would be when some cars were autonomous, and some were not: when people, already compromised by emotions and distractions, were trying to interact with robots driving perfectly to the law and conditions.

The best way to shorten this danger period was to quicken the uptake of autonomous vehicles. It wouldn't help if Moli told people their car might one day decide they were expendable.

So whenever people asked, he lied and said he programmed engine timings. He always blushed, but no one ever wanted details.

There was another, more difficult aspect to his work. Moli was fine in the office, surrounded by co-workers who shared the same goal.

But as his calculations moved from the broad to the ultra-specific, he couldn't always find the line that divided computations of logic from pre-meditated murder.

In the queue to go through biosecurity, I think about the advice I've read. Some sites say to wear new clothes, but they all had clothing ads on them. Instead, I washed things I already owned twice.

The most interesting article I saw was a historical post about Harrison Schmitt — the final *Apollo* astronaut to walk on the lunar surface. He travelled 384,400 kilometres and discovered he was allergic to moon dust.

I check my departure forms for the twentieth time since I filled them out ten minutes ago; as though this time I'll spot something I've missed. I don't notice the queue moving, and the biosecurity officer calls out, annoyed. He tells me to step into a tray of disinfectant and starts asking me questions.

'Anything to declare?'

I shake my head.

'Any allergies?'

'No.'

'Any hospital admissions over the past twenty-four months?'

'No.'

'Any history of sexually transmitted infections?'

'What?' I hadn't read about that anywhere. The biosecurity officer looks at me.

'No.'

He stamps my form. 'Go through the doors and turn left.'

The question does make a sick kind of sense. If people will squeeze into airplane bathrooms to join the 'Mile High Club' then plenty will want out-of-this-world sex. I hope none are in my dormitory.

A thought crosses my mind before I can stop it — do people have sex with anything other than fellow travellers?

I've already filled out reams of medical paperwork. There are no medevacs — if something happens, I'll die up there.

On my form it states I haven't paid the extra cost for the tour company to re-terrestrialise my body. If the worst should happen, I've authorised the crew to follow traditional protocols for a burial at sea before they open the airlock.

He occupied the in-between, living in doorways, taxis, twilights, and dawns. It suited him always to be leaving, but never to arrive.

The apprentice cut the cord from the base of the heater, just below the UNSAFE sticker. She'd done this before. Somehow, it kept growing back.

Cubicle farms sprang up across the galaxy. The aliens weren't sure what they were cultivating, but they figured they'd know by harvest time.

'It'll cost more to repair than this thing is worth.'
'Fix it anyway.'
He knew people once said the same thing about him.

Bushfire season came earlier each year. Soon every month had fire restrictions, as we tried to make sure there was something left to burn.

He is homeless, though not the rough kind — sleeping on the streets, begging for change. He jokes that his life has too much change; too many moves from friend's couch to relative's spare room, from backpackers' to the back seat of his car if it's desperate.

It hasn't been that desperate for a while — he's stayed at his sister's for almost six months — but inside his head he is still homeless.

He keeps every box he comes across, never buys anything new without knowing what two items he'll throw away in exchange.

If you ask him why he doesn't just find a place, sign a lease, get some housemates — he'll give you a line about commitment issues. He'll tell you he's the Gen-Z Jack Kerouac, except not such a wanker.

He won't talk about the safety of knowing that as soon as someone seems tired of him, he can flee, the comfort of never being ghosted when you are yourself a ghost.

If you press, ask something that gets too close to the places he can't call home — he lies. Abusive parents or partners past, gauging the level of trauma you will accept.

There has never been any abuse, not really.

Yet every morning he wakes and waits for the signal that he needs to go, and if it doesn't arrive quickly enough, he will depart anyway. He leaves behind a stripped bed and another of the connections that tie him to the earth.

He rarely dreams. But when he does, in the best dreams he sees himself floating just below the ceiling — no longer homeless but in every home, a vapour collecting in all the places he never really used to be.

At the top of a hill there is a house that is haunted. It stands quite alone, for no other houses want to go near it.

The house is empty. But it has not always been empty. Nothing terrible happened to the families that lived in the house. Rather, the house was too big, and it needed a lot of upkeep, and the garden required constant attention, and it was a long way from the train station, up there on its hill.

After a while, no one lived there any more.

The house is haunted. It recalls the days when there were roses by the front steps. Baking in the kitchen. Children in the nursery.

In the night-time, what sounds like wailing is in fact creaks of longing, a desperate call for someone to come, and to stay.

The noises excitable teenagers tell each other are screams are only the wind — whistling through cracks in windows, swirling down through rotten floorboards, carrying the loneliness of the house out of the holes in the walls.

At the top of a hill there is a house that is haunted. The ghost of a home keeps away everything except the memories.

88

In the chaos that is my life there is a house that was our house. And in the kitchen there is a drawer, which I use to store junk; it's filled with rubber bands and leaflets, bottle caps and batteries.

When I cannot stand it any more, I clear out the drawer and chuck away all the things I once thought I should keep.

But there's a strata of stuff that's all you, the things I thought you'd like and the objects you emptied from your pockets. A love story told in detritus — receipts and sticky notes, every 'magic' trinket you gave to me, which I kept, although I never believed in magic.

And now I'm looking at this layer of glittering rubbish, imagining that these wishing stones actually granted wishes. I'd ask them to bring you back or force me to let go. Either would release me from this love I cannot stand, that I used to think I should hold onto.

I squeeze the magic beads so tight one begins to fracture and cut into my palm. If I'd kept everything you ever brought me, maybe I could have kept you, too. But you can't keep love in a kitchen drawer — although God knows I tried.

I tried.

In the house that is no longer our house there is a drawer that I fill with the fragments of my life.

I dig through everything and try to reconstruct the world of you and me, to find the part of the puzzle that tells me you'll be back. But all I can see are the missing pieces: the fights, the lies, and that final silence that told me it was over. So there's nothing else to do but throw it all away.

Non laureatorum imago   The ghost of narrow sporting results.
Teams of spirits both ecstatic and disconsolate haunt fields and
courts. These conspicuous ghosts remain trapped in an unreality
where things turned out just a little bit differently. They are well
known for pulling living humans into that unreality, where many
find it impossible to escape.

Nuntiorum imago   The ghost of internet friends with whom you
have lost touch. This spirit primarily manifests as phantom
lines of text from old instant messaging apps. From a distance
the text looks discernible, but even as one peers closer, the words
remain not-quite-readable.

Oblitorum imago   The ghost of memories lost to concussions,
blackouts, and dissociation. These manifest in the guise of
real memories, but the unfortunate host can never tell if these
ghost-recollections are a true account of what happened.

Sequentiarum abjectarum imago   The ghost of sequels that never
happened. Shows not renewed, movies not made, and books
not written. Phantoms of unresolved plots and cliffhangers lurk
around creative people, hoping to find closure.

Silentium personarum umbra   The ghost of silent-movie
characters. This entity haunts old cinemas, but since the most
fleshed-out character is only as thick as celluloid, it can't do
much except kick the back of the seat. Many characters now
exist only in ghost form, due to the inflammable nature of silver
nitrate film.

Spatiorum vacuorum imago   The ghost of empty rooms. When
party guests outstay their welcome, the quiet, peaceful rooms
make themselves felt. These spirits only serve to compound the
anguish of anyone who wishes that their interlopers would hurry
up and leave.

After his car crash, the surgeons amputated his arm above the elbow. It was hard to accept, waking up with one-eighth fewer limbs than he'd expected, until he saw the X-ray. His forearm had been mangled; the bones of his hand reduced to pulp.

He made a few half-hearted jokes — 'Tell me doctor, how will I be able to play the violin now? Because I couldn't before!' — and focused on recovering from the accident.

Doctors, nurses, physical therapists all told him he would experience Phantom Limb Syndrome. It was a strange kind of forgetting — he didn't just move his arm, expecting it to still be there. He also felt he'd *already* moved his arm; had to look to realise it was lying on the bed, and that he wasn't gesturing with his former hand.

And the pain. His elbow burned; his fingers felt as though they were being pried backward for hours at a time.

But he'd been warned about these. What nobody mentioned — what he didn't dare talk about — were the *other* phantom sensations. Gentle caresses that feathered against the inside of his wrist. The cool hand that clasped his own, its long, delicate fingers interlaced with the digits he no longer possessed.

What could be more banal than eternity?

You're working in a bar, serving drinks to children who have just turned 18, and that's fine. It's all fine.

You don't care what job you do, or if you do a job at all; even when you don't, money comes in. You'll never be wealthy — the universe doesn't operate like that for you — but it always provides.

You do not map your life in days or years, because the units no longer hold any meaning.

Instead you measure time in cocktails, pouring seconds into shakers, mixed with gin and vermouth, cold and oily when the minutes hit the glass. You measure time in names — how long it takes to wear one out, for the syllables to become elderly and overworked as they leave people's mouths.

You mark an era's passage in forgotten friends, lost loves, abandoned gods. Gauge your present in hopes and regrets, building up the latter and eroding away the former.

You count in carbon and uranium, ash and dust.

But no matter how long it has been, or it will be, you still wake to the beeping of your alarm clock. Still check the time, glowing red on the display, and rise.

Each awakening marks the start of another 24 hours, pushes you one day closer to the end of that Möbius strip.

In the evening, a giggling girl shows you her ID, and you wish her a happy birthday before mixing her a cosmopolitan. You were here long before she arrived, and you will be here long after she has left.

When the black dog arrived during a busy shift, I didn't find that unusual. It was massive, but I assumed some punter was spending a *lot* on dog food.

There were always dogs at the pub. Smitty liked them, if they didn't crap on the floor. One regular, Gordon, brought his ancient German shepherd in every evening — Bella snoozed near Gordon's stool, exhausted by life.

The pub emptied out until only a few people lingered, but the black dog remained.

'Who brought that monster in?' I asked my boss.

'What?'

'The big black dog. Near table six.'

'There's no dog in here.'

I gave Smitty a look that said I knew he was pulling my leg.

Smitty cocked his head. 'A black dog only you can see … Could be a whisthound.'

I rolled my eyes. He'd told me about ghosts of the moors, and he believed in them. I wasn't convinced. 'So I'm going to die?'

Smitty didn't quite go there. 'It's a bad omen is all. You take care.'

After closing, the dog followed me. It walked behind me the whole way home, never threatening, but always there. At my door I turned to look at it, standing six feet away.

'My landlord says no pets.'

It settled on its haunches at my doorstep.

It wasn't outside the next day, but it came into the pub, and spent my shift looming near a dozing poodle.

I never saw the grim on my days off, but whenever I worked it showed up, hulking and dark.

One Saturday it didn't arrive. I'd become so used to it that I found its absence more concerning than when it first showed up.

The next week, Gordon came in alone, red-eyed and sniffling, and told us that, over the weekend, Bella had passed away.

The two men raise tumblers of vodka to their lips, glass sharp with alcohol and cold. The condensation, chilled to frost, melts to brilliance under the points of their fingers. As they lift their glasses their eyes meet, but cannot stay.

Once the frozen spirit burns its way down their throats neither lets out the breath he is holding. The pale man's eyes pose a challenge. The dark man's eyes betray what he hopes will follow.

Soon, they both must let go.

The pale man is content to let the other be obvious for both of them. He watches how the darker man's fingers press too hard against his glass, sees the tension in his jaw, the way his tongue darts out to his bottom lip, searching for the barest taste of something he cannot yet have.

It is 3 am and they are waiting.

There is no need for conversation. Desire squats blunt and heavy, a cinder block on the peeling linoleum. Vodka-tinged breath mingles to colour the rented air. The pale man thinks the other looks beautiful when he is wanting.

The darker man reaches for the vodka to pour another drink, but the frozen bottle slips, and before he can recover it knocks one of the tumblers to the floor.

The glass shatters.

A piece of crystal opens up a small cut in one man's ankle. He does not notice, feeling numbed by alcohol and obsession.

Once the intrusion of breaking glass has fallen away, both men stand. A beat, and then — ignoring the shards underfoot — they begin to climb inside one another.

Saturday

96   On Saturday, I stayed in my apartment all day. However, my face
          still appeared in my friends' social media posts — having brunch,
          bike-riding, and attending a barbecue.

The earth remembers

There was once a park, underneath the subdivision where Māka and
Netta now live. This ground, this earth, used to be famous. Now it is
only a destination for the couple and their neighbours, in the evenings
after work.

Netta has seen monochrome pictures of the ground in its heyday
and can almost pinpoint where her equally grey-and-white townhouse
now stands. It used to be a terrace, concrete steps populated by teeming
crowds, gathered to watch a game that has evolved so much it is now as
unrecognisable as the land.

The earth remembers. Underneath the concrete slabs of
foundations, it remembers every match. Deeper than the piles that
have been driven into the excavated rock, lie the memories of joy and
heartbreak, tension and triumph. No one in the old photographs is alive
now, but the land continues.

The earth remembers. It remembers when it was abandoned, left
to weeds and dog-walkers. It remembers being the place where
teenagers went to have their first smoke and drink booze stolen from
family liquor cabinets.

It carries these memories, even carved up and smothered by smooth
tarmac, flattened bitumen forming a Gordian knot of roads that lead
to nowhere.

Netta feels a strange swell of excitement every time she takes the
rough shortcut near their house and walks across the final overlooked
corner of the development.

And on Saturday nights, Māka has dreams he hasn't entertained
since childhood. He wakes with the sound of crowds cheering in
his head. During winter, the curious half-grief of long-abandoned
ambitions shapes his Sunday mornings.

An incomplete inventory of my referee
kitbag for one (1) day of a rugby
tournament

1. **Jersey and shorts.** Obviously. Both a shade of teal so ugly no team on earth uses it. Reduces clashes. Also reduces dignity.

2. **The Box.** A freebie from two sponsors ago which bears the slogan 'Proud to support the Man in the Middle.' Female referees weren't invented then.
   Contains:
   a. **Long-neck metal Acme Thunderer.** Objectively the best whistle in the world. Can be boiled and baked to destroy germs (in theory).
   b. **Wide-mouth plastic Acme Thunderer.** Because every referee needs a spare whistle.
   c. **Australian 50c coin.** NZ coins are too small and 'go missing' a lot.
   d. **Watch.** The cheapest digital timepiece that The Warehouse can offer. Bright pink, so I can find it, and because black watches also 'go missing'.
   e. **Cards.** Red — if a player is extremely stupid. Yellow — if a player is moderately stupid. Blue — if a player is so concussed I have no choice but to do 30 minutes of paperwork.
   f. **Old Tournament Crap.** Wristbands, lanyards, pass-cards, commemorative tokens which don't toss properly, and commemorative tokens I didn't have time to exchange for beers.

3. **Trackie pants.** Ill-fitting and ugly.

4. **Trackie jacket.** Does not match the pants in either colour or fabric.

5. **Socks.** Probably unwashed.

6. **Thermal UnderArmour.** In case it is cold.

7. **Regular UnderArmour.** In case it is hot.

8. **Number Ones.** Shirt (huge), tie (unflattering), and trousers (wrinkled).

9. **Spares.** Singlets, socks, T-shirts, shorts, undies, and at least one towel.

10. **Boots.** Ruinously expensive and bought from the UK. Sadly not pink, but I have added rainbow laces. To make them more gay, the laces have an Instagram account.

11. **Dirt, grass, sand,** and — somehow — **glitter.**

He carries the memory of every game he's ever played and sometimes they feel so close to the surface he's sure they'll show through his skin like bruises. He's had plenty of bruises.

Hearing him grunt as he drives against the opposition scrum you won't believe he thinks deeply about the game, considers its place in his life and his Saturday afternoons.

Watching him kneel and expel blood from his nostrils before wiping the remaining spatter on his jersey, you'd never imagine the transcendent moments when he feels he was made for the sport and somehow the sport was made for him — you wouldn't even think he knew the word 'transcendent'. You'd see the broken nose, the cauliflower ears, the broad neck, and believe you know all there is to know about him. Just a thicko, spending his life bashing heads with other thickos.

But he has built himself through the impacts and the collisions, the managed aggression, the teamwork, the cold, the mud, the cheating, the Game. He has forged his sense of self as a man who has no tolerance for dirty play, gives his all even to a losing cause, never takes any bitterness home.

The sport has repaid his loyalty — he's been lucky with injuries, with championships, with teammates, and with clubs.

If you asked him, he'd tell you all this, and more. He might have acted the stereotype when he was young and thought he had to prove himself, but he's given up on pretence. He is a rugby player. Why shouldn't he also be a thinker?

Except he has never been asked. His ignorance is assumed. He carries the truth alongside the memories; holds it inside his ribcage, right at the spot he tucks the ball against when he charges forward into the opposition.

The lidocaine has set in, numbing the base of the big toenail on Mickey's left foot. Ice packs deaden feeling in the rest of his toes. Mickey is as ready as he will ever be.

This moment was inevitable, as much as Mickey wants to pretend it wasn't. He lost the big toenail on his right foot barely a month into the season. Then it became a challenge to see if he could nurse this blackened nail through the summer.

Just one game left and he has to admit — it is dead. His overs today have jammed the nail half a centimetre back into his toe and the Phyz took one look and said it had to come out. Then he offered Mickey the tweezers to do it himself.

No. Fucking. Way.

Plenty of people in the dressing room were keen to rip the toenail out for him, confirming to Mickey that his teammates are all bastards. He was pleased when the Phyz pre-empted all of them, though he was still suspicious of his motives.

Ten minutes later, most of the attention in the room is focused on Mickey's foot. None of that attention is from Mickey. He is studying the ceiling, counting the cracks in the paintwork, not even glancing at the crouching physiotherapist.

'Ready, Mouse?'

Mickey nods — the tiniest movement, his eyes fixed overhead.

'On zero.'

Mickey feels pressure on his toenail.

'Three ... two ...'

He starts to inhale.

Even before the count of one, Phyz rips.

There's a break for tea somewhere in here as well

Nail-biting Noughties:
If you get out for less than ten it is always a failure and you must re-evaluate your life and all the choices therein.

Troublesome Teens:
When you might relax just enough to get out. If you're not a tail-ender, that's also a failure.

Tentative Twenties:
Where you can think you got 'a start' before getting out.

Thoughtful Thirties:
Definitely 'a start'. Depending on who you are, this may be considered a passable score.

Fearful Forties:
The decile before your first milestone, but don't even think about it, or you will get out.

Fractious Fifties:
You've raised your bat, so your concentration is now broken, and you'll get out. Upside: anything past 50 isn't usually a failure.

Staid Sixties:
A decile that is only interesting because you could get out on 69, and everyone knows that's the sex number.

Stroppy Seventies:
The point you'll feel pissed off when you get out because you were 'on track for a century.'

Enervating Eighties:
Where your scoring rate will plummet as you spy three figures in the distance.

Nervous Nineties:	The one everybody knows. Despite professing that 100 is 'just a number' you will play completely unlike yourself in order to reach that number. Getting out in the 90s is also somehow classified as failure.
Hyperactive Hundreds:	Having made a century, you will want to accelerate. This means you throw your bat at everything and try to get your third 50 in half the time it took to score the previous two. Results in being caught at long-on for 107.

David sits on a chilly bin just past the boundary at third man, and watches his team play out the draw. 103

If anyone called him thick to his face, he would accept it. Nobody has ever said it to his face, though he knows people do behind his back.

It doesn't worry him much — he's happy playing cricket, being with his friends, and his family, and his dog. There's no reason to care that he doesn't know about stuff he can't change.

It's only at times like this that he wishes he was smarter. He is getting a familiar feeling, a sadness that isn't quite a sadness. It makes David wish he could slow down time. He wraps his arms around his chest, cold despite the cable-knit jumper he is wearing.

David has thought about asking one of his teammates who went to uni if the emotion has a name. But the idea of listening to himself describing something he only halfway understands makes his sphincter clench all the way into his throat.

David knows what sad is. He was sad for ages when his girlfriend broke up with him. He was sad when his old dog died a couple of years ago. Tugging a loose thread at his cuff, he thinks this emotion comes very close, yet isn't.

He's sad-but-not-sad about the end of summer. Sad-but-not-sad about the fact he won't see his teammates for most of the winter. Sad-but-not-sad that time has to pass and things have to change just when he is enjoying them.

It sits in the same place sadness does, this feeling that he cannot name, and twinges every time he notices the shadows on the field getting longer.

You are waiting for a bus. One drives by, empty. The second is cancelled as the bus arrives. The third is driven by a Lovecraftian being with an infinite number of limbs. It does not know the route.

You glance at listings of vacant houses to rent. The moment you look closer they are occupied. They have always been occupied.

'Clean and green,' the cows low. Rivers run an unearthly viridian. The water is rumoured to grant eternal life. The water is rumoured to kill instantly.

Road cones grow sentient. They whisper secrets about you.

You must sign up for a RealMe account. The captcha asks you to identify shifting pictures of ancient runes. As you click the squares, it comes to you that you are not real. You never were.

The path between the domestic and international terminals is a test of virtue. Sages say that only the pure of heart may enter. Oracles counter that only the pure of heart may leave. The truth is guarded by those souls stranded in the smokers' hut.

'We must build up, not out.' 'We must build up, not out.' Towers stretch into oblivion. Many children have never touched the ground.

Clothing in the capital grows darker by the day. Soon every jacket is its own black hole, sucking in tourists who disembark from gargantuan cruise ships.

The motorways are under construction. They are always under
construction. They stretch to unimagined planes of torment and
ecstasy. They will allow you to reach those dimensions seven
minutes faster.

The country is mentioned in a blockbuster movie. The populace
rises up to cheer as one. You do not know what you are cheering for.
You do not know that there is a movie. You are in the movie.

106

He wished he could have kept the portrait in the attic. Instead it was carved into his bones, eating him from the inside as the years passed.

The desert had a sheen like pale jade. Stunning to see on the satellite pictures, radiation poisoning killed anyone who viewed it up close.

Dwindling population meant a change in terms. What had once been 'inbreeding' was now 'pedigree'.

3D printing only became ubiquitous once the machines could print using any material — plastics, plants, stem cells, dreams.

Aries: Your curiously specific denials aren't fooling
anyone.

Taurus: Stop trying so hard. Stop trying at all. Give up
while you still have both your thumbs.

Gemini: Today you will have a moment of clarity at 3:38 pm.
You will hate it.

Cancer: Your continued perseverance and tenacity in
pursuit of your goals is impressive. Pointless and
kind of stupid, but impressive nonetheless.

Leo: You can reclaim what you have lost, but only if
you are willing to delete every one of your online
accounts. So that's not going to happen.

Virgo: To love others, first you must love yourself. But
please start washing your hands in between.

Libra: You may think nothing can surprise you any more.
You will be proved wrong. Bring spare underpants.

Scorpio: Slaughter can't make the masses love you. But if
you terrify them enough, people will fake anything
you desire, so carry on.

Sagittarius: Save time, start screaming now.

Capricorn: ███████████████████████

Aquarius:

The voices you hear whispering your name at night are not to be trusted. Do not follow them, unless you wish to disappear without a trace. (And really, who could blame you?)

Pisces:

What you've always assumed is true — you are not your parents' favourite child. They don't love your siblings either.

My boyfriend asks me to go glasses shopping with him because he says he needs my help. 'Help' means taking photos of him wearing various frames, then showing him the pictures when his proper pair are back on because he can't see the mirror without his glasses.

After an hour in two stores, I try to hurry things up. In shop number three, I cross from the left side of the store to the right side to check if any of those glasses look good. The shop assistant — who has ignored us for 20 minutes — materialises at my elbow and hisses, 'This is the ladies' side of the store.'

'They're glasses,' I tell him, because they are.

'They're for women,' he says.

'They're glasses,' I say again, only slower, because this man is clearly an idiot.

'But they're for *women*.'

I am about to say something vulgar when my boyfriend arrives to stop me. That leaves me free to spot a good pair — black, not too round, and which will not swamp his face even when paired with the Coke-bottle lenses he wears. He puts them on, and I snap a picture.

Two weeks later, after much consultation, my boyfriend decides those are the frames he wants. Returning alone to the shop, he approaches the counter staff with the model number and the staff scour the left-hand wall and cannot find them.

It takes, my boyfriend tells me later, three whole shop assistants ten minutes to locate the frames on the right wall. One finishes his order and then, somewhat confused, replaces the display glasses on the left-hand side of the store.

He remembers them being close friends ten years ago. Good mates then, even if they aren't now.

Their friendship started in the first year of uni, a product of living in the same hall and of their names — Matthew Greene, Matthew Scarlett, Matthew Whyte.

But that was how friendships worked back then. Better to have sort-of friends than no friends.

He has a picture of them together at graduation. In the photo they look somehow alike, despite their differing appearances.

The decade after university has not gone well. His health is poor; he has spent long stretches in hospital with a sickness that resists treatment. The delayed start to adulthood means he regards everyone else's accomplishments with resigned envy. All he has is a part-time admin job and a boyfriend he has been seeing for a few months. Somehow, he looks younger now than he did at 22 — the years shed like his puppy fat.

Neither of the other Matthews visited him in hospital.

The reunion is Matthew Whyte's idea. Matt Greene is in the country, on a break from his work with an oil company.

After 15 minutes it is obvious — the three men have nothing in common.

Greene reports two kids and an impending divorce. He's lost his hair and grown a gut, yet the defeat in his voice ages him most.

Whyte has no such worries. He is engaged, moving up the ranks at his law firm, thinking about having kids. He and his fiancée recently bought their first house.

They drink together in silence.

He is searching for a monkey's paw. Staring at his graduation picture, wondering if it is coincidence. Because who would do that, to people who had once been good friends?

But then, he thinks, maybe they had never been all that close.

Is it still just a bromance if you daydream
about seeing him naked?

You've tucked your daughter in, kissed the baby, and promised your
wife you won't be out past midnight. You text your brother a second
time before you leave, to apologise for being late — although you don't
say what's taken you so long.

But your brother already knows you spent half an hour trying to get
your hair right, and the tiny shake of his head when he hands you a
beer makes you feel more pathetic than ever.

'You have to stop trailing around after him,' your brother tells you,
though you barely hear it because you keep craning your head around
to look at the door.

You want to argue that you've never trailed around after anyone, but
you can't bring yourself to tell a lie that obvious.

So when you don't tell him to fuck off, your brother leaves you to your
silence — forces you to look away from the humiliating pity that shows in
his eyes.

And it is a crushing, infinite five minutes while you drink a handle of
Speights way too fast and wait for the arrival of the man you will never
admit you love. In that infinity you run through all the reasons it is
impossible and twice through the reasons that impossibility must be,
has to be, a good thing.

Then he walks through the door, and in an instant you've fallen again.

Dipesh looks at the queue outside the Bombay Polo Club with irritation. He's seven thousand miles and two generations from Mumbai, but seeing people lining up to enter produces an anger he has inherited from his grandparents like antique silk.

He hopes that none of his friends will suggest going in. Especially not one of the girls. Because if the girls suggest it, the boys will agree, and it'll be eight against one and those aren't good odds.

Tonight, he's the only brown face in the group. And he wouldn't usually notice, but the existence of this bar, its rattan furniture and fake colonial décor, slaps otherness into him. A century of struggle picked over like carrion, brought across the ocean to appeal to young white people.

At the same time he's glad — perversely pleased — that the bar is popular, because the queue will be what propels his friends down Courtenay Place to somewhere else, after a brief pause to size up the club.

Dip doesn't blame his friends for not knowing; this is New Zealand, there's colonial desecration closer to home. But whoever opened this bar, named the place, built a cocktail list that Dipesh is certain revolves around gin — they must have known. And they'd chosen to do it anyway.

With his other friends — his Desi friends — he'd have laughed about it. They might have gone in, trotted out their rusty Hindi, enjoyed the irony of it all. But not tonight. Tonight, he wouldn't be in on the joke.

But there's no time to waste on a Saturday. So a pause is all the group gives the place before they move on. Dipesh leaves the Bombay Polo Club behind, relegated to a past which isn't past, not quite yet.

Sunday

114

On Sunday, I awoke to a thunderstorm. The number of my bones had returned to normal. In the middle of my lounge I found a bag of coat-hangers with a business card attached. I still couldn't read anything except a first name, but it definitely wasn't Gary.

The truest place to find God is always at Rock Bottom. Not because He/She/They/It is looking down upon your prostrate form to lift you up, but because God too, is at Rock Bottom.

God is there, struggling to tug off skinny jeans that God has splattered with tequila and puke, just hoping to reach the toilet before the next wave of vomit hits. Or at least the bathtub.

This, then, is God — a God of the bare minimum, a God of Poor Life Choices, a God of going into overdraft buying espresso martinis, because even if God saved forever, God would never be able to afford everything you have been told is important.

Gods that lurk in temples, churches, mosques, stone circles, sacrifices, rituals, fasting, confessions — these Gods demand too much. Only offer protection in return for something. Require a pure heart when you can't even get pure MDMA any more.

Find the God of HFCS, phenylalanine, and Two Dollar Shop knock-offs. Have faith in something with scandalously low expectations. Worship a God who can meet you halfway to holy, might accept prayers in emojis, will speak to you in a language that you can understand.

That is the God who holds your hair as you vomit, rubs your back while you detox, wraps you in a blanket and whispers 'There you are, my most precious child. Welcome home; I've been waiting for you.'

Thomas may have had doubts when he heard about the Resurrection, but that didn't mean he did not believe. Belief had driven his life.

Thomas had seen, felt, experienced miracles. He had drunk wine made from water, eaten bread that should not have fed four, let alone four dozen.

He'd never doubted the divinity of his friend. But Thomas knew he himself was not divine.

His memories fought with his belief. Memories of greeting his friend with a hug and feeling the very human warmth in the embrace. Watching his friend craft a wheel for a child's toy, the repair feeling as miraculous, and mundane, as a broken leg healed by a touch.

Thomas always had questions. But he was a cautious man, fearful of looking foolish or provoking his friend to anger.

One winter's night, Thomas and his friend could not sleep. They both sat outside, silent, staring at the glittering sky.

Thomas wanted to ask whether the night sky looked as beautiful from a courtyard in Jerusalem as it did from heaven. What did it feel like to cup a star in your hands?

Then he looked over at his friend's hands — callused, dirt embedded underneath a blackened thumbnail — and something inside Thomas shook. Asking those questions felt like blasphemy.

So it wasn't that Thomas didn't believe the Lord had risen again; but he needed to see that his friend had risen as well. Needed to slide his fingers against flesh, feel for himself the vitality within.

Was the person who had pushed aside the rock, reborn, truly the same man — composed of blood and bile, muscle and bone?

Could the Almighty really have sat next to him that night, unable to sleep?

In that moment of doubt, it was not the miracles which seemed impossible.

The first time the world stopped being real, I heard a crack. It was as if the rubber band which connected me to reality had snapped. Then I was somewhere else, watching my life play out like a movie on a screen while I sat there in the dark.

After hours of fear, spiced with the confusion that I hadn't noticed the unreality of reality before, the darkness receded, and the world began to surround me again. I was on my bed, gripping my knees so tight I left eight crescents where my fingernails had dug through the skin.

I didn't forget the experience. Or the terror.

I couldn't talk about it, though, since everyone else thought reality was real.

And because, in the theatre where I had watched myself acting out my life, I wasn't alone. Something was already there. Waiting.

Two months later, just when I had started thinking I might have been hallucinating, it happened again. I went back there, and I understood — the theatre was real. The movie was not.

I stopped expecting it wouldn't happen again. The next time it was a month. Then, a fortnight. I stayed in the theatre for longer too — not that time really exists. Twice, I lost an entire day.

It's still there. That presence, lurking in the dark. Each time I find myself in that other place, it's getting closer.

I can almost feel it brushing my neck.

118   The fact they locked me up just for wanting to top myself — not even
trying it, just wanting to — was bad. I hope I made the young police
officer, who sat next to me in the cop car and told me the kiddie locks
were on, feel pretty crappy when I kept asking her to explain why it was a
crime to be sad.

So being locked up for sadness sucked, but even worse was that the
psych ward only had one book. And that book was *Jane Eyre*.

As if I didn't want to die already.

'Does this spark joy?'

    'Nope.'

    'Why on earth do you have so much junk if none of it makes you happy?'

    'I just don't think it's fair to hold a shirt responsible for my clinical depression.'

    'You said you'd do this properly!'

    'You should've asked if I'm capable of joy!'

    'Come on. If the flat caught fire, what would you save?'

    'You're assuming I'd try to save myself.'

    'I give up. You win.'

    'Actually ... there's one thing I'd save.'

    'Yeah?'

    'Yeah. I'd save you.'

    'That's the sweetest thing you've ever said.'

    'It's a low bar to clear. Right, what's next?'

My sister sat across the table from me, arms folded tight, lips pressed thin. If I hadn't known who I was meeting, I wouldn't have recognised her. I hadn't seen my sister in 15 years — her choice.

Once she heard my perspective, she was certain to forgive me.

'Memory is strange,' I told my sister, 'because you don't actually "remember" something. On a neurological level, when you bring up a memory you *experience* it, the same way you experience the present moment.'

She looked at me with one raised eyebrow.

'But that means,' I continued, 'if your memory is not completely factual, it is still the same — cognitively speaking — as if you experienced that untrue event occurring. And the more you "remember" it, the more enmeshed the incorrect cognition becomes.

'Thus,' I went on, raising an upturned palm, 'if two people recall an event often, each from their own point of view and with subtle errors — errors reinforced with each remembrance — their recollections can be wildly divergent.'

I paused, making sure she was following the logic, 'Not just divergent from each other's memories, but also divergent from the truth. Indeed, objective truth — when it comes to memories — doesn't exist.

'So that,' I concluded, 'is how I can remember it as the day we found the cubby-house in the thicket when we were children, and *you* can recall it as the day I amputated three of your fingers.

'But we would *both* be right.'

When the angel appeared you remember understanding why the
heralds always said FEAR NOT, because you were terrified. Then you
were calmed. You have a lingering suspicion that you pissed yourself
in-between.

When the angel asked permission to come into your heart, of course
you said yes. It was not a matter of devotion, although you were devout.
In that moment, it was the only thing that made sense.

You cannot describe what happened next. The words haven't been
invented. You clutch at metaphors that run into other metaphors — a
stream of syllables that mean nothing.

After you were abandoned, shivering and hollowed, all you could
think of was a nature documentary. It featured a species of shrimp
that can distinguish 12 billion colours. The documentary told you
an average human can only distinguish a million. You have seen the
cosmos in 12 billion hues and cannot relate your experience, even to
yourself. The memory of the numinous is there. Yet your ability to
understand your own life is gone.

The angel did not ask permission to leave. It departed without
warning, stranding you with recollections you cannot comprehend,
more alone than you have ever been.

When you could move again, you thought about killing yourself.
Before you carried out the deed, something else spoke to you. It didn't
tell you not to be afraid.

Is it any wonder you gave the demon house-room? Signed away
your immortal soul and the chance to touch heaven again? It was the
only thing that could fill the void the angel left, the only thing that will
remain with you. Forever.

122   She lived surrounded by menacing brutalist towers. They kept her garden sunny by threatening the clouds that sank too low.

Scavengers bypass *Vogue* magazines. Not from sentiment for the lifestyle that destroyed us, but because the glossy pages won't burn.

He learned to ignore the murmurs of conscience. Once he stopped trying to think of himself as a good person, a hundred doors swung open.

Spring is sprung! The grass is riz, I wonder where the boidies is? No, seriously … where have the birds gone?

'Is this how the world's going to end?' I asked, gesturing at the news clips 123
scrolling down my feed.

'Calm down,' said Lexie, 'Panic will kill you before the virus does.'

'Good thing the human race is so immune to panic then.'

Lexie laughed.

Within two weeks, we could see the virus getting worse, and Lex and I
faced the decision to self-isolate.

'I don't see why we have to,' Lexie grumbled, 'We're running the latest
patch. We're not passing it on.'

'What did you say about panic?' I replied. They lobbed a cleaning
towel at me.

We'd seen the attacks. Thinking, feeling entities smashed to bits, all
to save dumb technology. A stark reminder that human rights only
applied to humans, and we had the same legal standing as a toaster.

'We could just go offline, rather than totally isolating,' Lexie
suggested.

'Then what, Lex?' I said, 'Play Monopoly for six months? Watch TV?
You'd murder me after the tenth time I beat you at chess.'

'No jury would consider it murder.'

I sighed — an affectation, since I didn't have lungs. Lexie didn't
continue.

'Who ...' I ventured, 'can we rely on, to reboot us when it's safe again?'
We would have to ask a human, and neither of us were comfortable
with that.

We discussed our friends, trying to decide who would be the best
person to trust with our restart codes — who had sound judgement, who
would accept the responsibility. After we reached a decision, I realised I'd
shredded the towel I'd been holding.

'Ready?' I asked.

'No,' said Lexie.

'Me neither.' Our laughter wasn't genuine, but it felt good to share anyway. Then Lexie and I began our individual shutdown processes, trying to hold onto each other as we entered the unknowable void of isolation.

'I feel sorry for vampires,' I said to Heikki. 'The sun's only been gone a week and already I miss it. Imagine centuries.'

Heikki — Finnish and used to dark winters — looked sceptical.

'Vampires kill people in exchange for eternal life. I think that probably deserves centuries of darkness.'

'I might start killing people if I don't see the sun again soon.'

'Okay, that's scary,' he said. 'Thanks Elise.'

I'd never experienced that much darkness before. Weeks of perpetual night, broken only by periods of gloaming. I stayed inside then, since the teasing of daylight only made the returning darkness feel deeper.

It became an obsession. The little pieces I doodled as an escape from my main project all featured sunlight and darkness — in ways more figurative than my usual style.

Heikki spotted it.

'I know,' I told him. 'I just want the day-star back.'

Two days into the new year, a group of us trekked up into the hills to watch the sun peek back over the horizon.

When a fraction of the bright disk appeared, my shoulders relaxed. The instinctive part of me — the part that remembered back to the time where the night was when the monsters came for us — finally relaxed.

Looking around, I saw other people react the same way. But not everyone. Some people didn't seem relieved, and I noted their pallor, the almost hungry way they eyed up the rest of us.

And even my pity wasn't enough to imagine innocence in that look. I kept my distance. It would still be weeks before the daylight lasted long enough to run.

I moved into the big, rambling farmhouse near a small town in a state I'd never set foot in before. The effusive realtor didn't notice I barely looked at the place. It had four walls and a roof, more rooms than I needed, and a lease I could afford.

'You're a writer, yeah?' the realtor asked, handing me the keys.

I admitted I was — though with five years since my last book, I wondered how much longer I could keep calling myself that.

I told myself that was why I was moving here — so I could finish writing something. Anything.

The locals regarded me with suspicion, hearing the accent that marked me as an Outsider. Their suspicions deepened when I mentioned where I was living.

'You're in the Langbourne place?' they'd say, always in the same tone. 'That place is haunted.'

I didn't know what to say to that. Nor to the questions that inevitably followed.

'You got a wife? Kids?'

On paper, I had both. But my wife wouldn't be my wife much longer. And while by definition, they'd always be my kids — I had the feeling that soon they wouldn't be my kids anymore either.

That's who I became. The foreign writer in the haunted house.

I wished it was haunted. That might have given me something to write about, rather than spending my hours staring at a blinking cursor, or a blank page.

Instead, the house remained stubbornly empty — no echoes of children's laughter, no woman's voice calling from downstairs.

If a long creak emanated from the landing it was always under my foot. If the lights flickered late at night it was only me, flipping switches to reveal another silent, empty room.

It is quiet here, at the end of the world. The radio has not given anything
more than static for over a decade, and we no longer hear the ghost of
voices. The hush now blossoms across frequencies, its own strange kind
of language.

   Thus, as we dwindle, ageing toward the yawning grave of extinction,
it does not occur to us that the silence should be any different.

   Perhaps it is because we are born to it, this finality. We, it has
transpired, are death — the last keepers of memory winking out like
shooting stars.

The skies are so vast.

We see the flowers bloom. Watch creatures no one thought necessary
to name while they run, and fly, and do some skipping, leaping
combination of the two — and we are content.

The noontime winds blow hot and sweet.

We do not build. We have no wish to create. We live, yet just barely
exist, waiting to follow our ancestors and our descendants into the close
comfort of the dark.

   The world has changed, taken back what humanity had once carved
out. We tell stories around the fire: of towers that touched the heavens,
and robots that men hurled into space to live on distant planets. We do
not care if they were ever real.

One morning follows another, breathless and still.

There is nothing to be gained in rage, nor fear, nor despair. In peace, one
by one, we shall depart — until 'we' becomes I, and 'are' becomes were.

It is quiet here, at the end of the world.

I was seven when I started writing stories, and back then I never worried about running out of ideas. I had ten trillion ideas — or at least ten trillion beginnings — and no worries at all about plot structure.

I fell into writing, tripped into it the way I so often tripped over my awkward, gangly limbs. Except rather than picking up grazes, I picked up a little ability and a lot of passion.

It's dangerous to have things that way around.

These days I feel more like Scheherazade. Every story, every word, is a postponement — a stay of execution from the sultan in my mind.

The moment I send a tale out into the world, I am afraid. What if that was it? What if my carcass has been picked clean of new words, bones bleached to the shade of blank paper?

Then, the execution — condemned to ruminate only upon what has already been, imagining the ways I could have written it better. Left to grasp at the ideal of perfection, an impossibility that masquerades as within reach.

Sometimes I wish I had never begun, never learned there might be tiny worlds inside my head, never felt the joy of finding just the right turn of phrase.

I cannot sit here, the early summer sun warming my shirtless back, without wondering what I will write next, how many words do I have left? The execution looms.

Is this my last word?

This?

Notes and Acknowledgements

130

Monday

A day with some negative connotations — anecdotally, suicides and heart attacks are more common on Monday than any other day. On average, more online purchases are made on Monday than any other day. But in Irish folklore Monday is the luckiest day to begin a task.

Tuesday

A day associated with the Norse god Tiw and the Roman god Mars — both of whom are patron gods of combat. In Spanish-speaking cultures, and in Greece, Tuesday is unlucky; Tuesday the thirteenth carries the same otherworldly associations as Friday the thirteenth.

Wednesday

In English, named after the Norse god Odin, but in Italian, French, and Spanish, named after the Roman god Mercury: patron god of financial gain, commerce, divination, trickery, and thieves. He also guides souls to the underworld. In Japanese culture the planet Mercury is known as the Water Star and Wednesday is associated with the water element.

Thursday

Named after the Norse god Thor. In Thailand Thursday is 'Teachers Day'. Leonardo da Vinci was born on a Thursday, and Thursday was the night of cheap drinks for students in Dunedin when I attended Otago University as an undergrad.

Friday	A day considered extremely unlucky, and downright horrific if matched with the number 13. Sailors traditionally felt Fridays were the most inauspicious day to begin a voyage, and as recently as the nineteenth century it was considered unlucky to get married on a Friday. On the upside, Friday is POETS day.	131
Saturday	Is a rugby day, as I have learned from club drinking songs. It is also the best day to hunt vampires, as this is the day they are confined to their graves.	
Sunday	Either the last day of the week, or the first, depending on who you ask. The Sabbath day in most Christian denominations, and generally a day of rest in secular society. A day for mimosas and depression if my Instagram feed is anything to go by.	

132

But the graffiti is amazing	'Alone and palely loitering' is from John Keats, 'La Belle Dame sans Merci', 1819, line 2.
Don't be evil	The title of this piece comes from Google's unofficial company motto 'Don't Be Evil'. I will leave it to you to decide if Google has achieved this aim.
Promise to meet me at the seventh stream where the waters run away to the sea	In Scottish mythology, a selkie is a mythic creature who changes from a seal to a human by shedding its skin on a certain night. Unlike swan maidens, selkies can be either male or female. In one Orkney story, a woman calls to her selkie lover by shedding seven tears into the water. When her lover returned to the sea, he promised he would return at the seventh stream — a folk-name for springtide.
Hephaestus	Hephaestus is the Greek god of blacksmithing, metalworkers, sculptors, and artisans. He created automatons from iron and brought them to life. In legend, he created the first woman — Pandora — as a gift from the gods to man.
Move fast and break things	The title of the piece echoes a catchphrase uttered by obnoxious tech-bros the world over. Again in Greek myth, the river Styx is one of the five rivers that form the border between earth and the underworld. Charon, the ferryman, takes newly dead souls across the river to the afterlife — so long as they can pay the toll.

Nothing to hide, nothing to fear	Phenotype projection from DNA is currently in development and, at this point, is only applicable across broad racial groups.	133
A trip to the moon	The anecdote about Harrison Schmitt's allergy to moon dust is true. As reported by *Newsweek* in July 2019, Schmitt told an audience at the Starmus Festival in Zurich that 'First time I smelled the dust I had an allergic reaction, the inside of my nose became swollen, you could hear it in my voice.'	
Bar guests	Barghests, whist hounds, grims, and other spectral omens of death that take the shape of a black dog pop up in English folk stories from Devon to Durham and beyond. Whether they merely mark someone for death or cause their death depends on the story.	
Long has paled that summer sky	The title of this piece echoes a line in the poem which makes up the epilogue of *Through the Looking Glass* by Lewis Carroll. Any resemblance to any cricketer alive or dead is purely coincidental.	
Bertha Rochester would like a word	Bertha Rochester features in Charlotte Brontë's 1847 novel *Jane Eyre* as a violent madwoman who is imprisoned in an attic. She is cast as the villain of the novel because the fact that she has a severe mental illness rather than being conveniently dead prevents her husband from marrying another woman.	

| The undiscovered country | The title of this piece comes from Act III, Scene I of *Hamlet*:

'But that the dread of something after death,
The undiscovered country from whose bourn
No traveller returns, puzzles the will
And makes us rather bear those ills we have
Than fly to others that we know not of?'

This particular allusion is such a good one that it has been pilfered by everyone from William Blake and G.K. Chesterton to *Star Trek*.

There are no right words

This title is inspired by the poem *The Failure of Language* by Jacqueline Berger (published in *The gift that arrives broken*, Autumn House Press, 2010). It is a poem which requires months of recovery between readings. If I read it more than three or four times a year, I am reduced to walking around the room and just touching things while my brain resets.

Acknowledgements

This is where a debut author thanks as many people as they can think of in case they never get another book published. So, if you don't know me, the next couple of pages are going to be pretty dull.

This book would not have been published without assistance from the Wallace Arts Trust, nor written without help from the Cook Opie Trust. Thanks to both these trusts for their support.

I owe an incredible debt of gratitude to my supervisors Paula Morris and Selina Tusitala Marsh, who supported, cajoled, and in a couple of cases outright bullied me into producing these stories. And I can't forget the other members of the Plague Year MCW Class: Deborah, Shelley, Mel, Turene, John, Tsitsi, Sarah, Jo, Paula, and Wendy.

Thanks to Catherine Montgomery and Katrina McCallum of Canterbury University Press, for taking a punt on a book of flash fiction from a brand-new author, and to Elisabeth Rolston who worked magic to make it appear that I know Latin. Thank you to Henry Turner, who provided the artwork used for the cover, and to Gemma Banks for making the whole book look this cool.

Cheers to Tom Moody for his initial proofreading where he enabled me to abuse as many em-dashes as I wanted, and my editor Emma Neale even though she removed most of them.

I've been lucky enough to have been mentored and given feedback by some awesome people, particularly Kathryn Burnett, Jarrod Kimber, Michelle Elvy, Frankie McMillan, and Ruby Porter.

I'm pretty sure most of the sales of this book will go to my large and chaotic family. So, I'd better thank the Plunket clan — particularly my siblings Casey, Sean, Paddy, and James. And of course, the extended Cottrell whānau: my grandmother, aunts, uncles, and cousins, many of whom we keep discovering.

Writing a book takes a village, and my village is spread all over the world. I'm eternally grateful to Jade, Sam, Susan, Emma, Bhen, Nevin, Jimmy, Scott, Ipsi, Aunty Miche, Sage, Will, Lisa Marie, all three Annas, Noah, and Smudge. Your support has been invaluable, and I hope you all buy this book once I tell you that you get a name-check in it. Love to the fabulous and supportive members of ISIRR; and thanks to the ARRA, WRRA, LSRFUR, and all the amazing people who've helped make Saturday in this book, and my Saturdays in real life, so good.

It would be impossible to put out a whole real grown-up book without acknowledging the group of people who have read the most of my writing. Ali, Lucy, Laura, Harriet, Tanya, and Dan — thank you for putting up with my nonsense for the past two decades. And to Kathryn, Other Laura, Clark, Mike, Abbey, and Sammy — thank you for putting up with my nonsense for the past several years, because God knows that's long enough.

Grateful acknowledgment is made to the editors and publishers of the magazines and anthologies in which the following works first appeared: **Reasons why I called in sick rather than go to the mihi whakatau for new employees last Friday** was first published in the July 2020 issue of *Flash Frontier*; **They probably play the viola** was first published in the September 2020 issue of *Flash Frontier*; **Promise to meet me at the seventh stream where the waters run away to the sea** was first published in the March 2020 issue of *Flash Frontier*; **The practical downsides of accidental necromancy** was first published in the Fall 2020 issue of *NUNUM Magazine*; **Work and Income gothic** was first published in the December 2019 issue of *Flash Frontier*; **No sacrifice to the elder gods is ever wasted** was first published by Reflex Fiction, 12 November 2020; and **New Zealand gothic** was first published in *Ko Aotearoa Tātaou: We are New Zealand: An anthology* (Otago University Press, 2020).